In The Beginnir

Nestled on the outskirts of a village, within the heart of the Cotswold's, (an area of outstanding natural beauty), surrounded by rolling hills dotted with sheep, meadows, and woodlands in a relaxed almost sleepy atmosphere lay a Cottage built out of mild yellow limestone, often described as being golden or honey in appearance, with a stone roof, and dry stone walls that surround the grounds of the cottage. This is the home of Elliot, his two sisters (Scarlett and Abigail Summer), and their father (George Summer).

The house has a traditional look with an oak door to the front, and oak sash windows. There is a small front garden filled with the most beautiful flowers, Lavender, chamomile, primrose, honeysuckle, and Clematis flowers climbing up the walls. The smell of the flowers is beautiful.

There is a garden to the rear, which is long and meadow-like, with the odd apple tree here and there, and a chicken coop. And at the bottom of the garden is a wall of great oak trees, stretching up to the sky, with the greenest of leaves. The leaves glisten in the morning sun. The garden is almost silent, apart from the sound of the odd robin, and the hum of the bumble bees as they fly from flower to flower to drink the flower's sweet nectar, pollinating as they go. The garden is one that you could quite happily sit back in a chair and absorb the sun's rays in.

The house inside has a cozy, snug feel to it, enhanced by the open burning fire. The embers from the fire burn with a distinctive red, almost orange glow. Smoke rises from the embers and disappears up, inside the stone chimney breast. The flames appear as though they are dancing, as they flicker around. The glow and movement of the flames cast moving shadows of the furniture onto the stone walls. The room has two small sofas, both of which draped with patchwork blankets. And on the windowsill is a red vase, filled with freshly cut sunflowers.

The kitchen is stone paved, with oak-carved units along two walls, and a carved oak table and chairs in the middle of the floor. There is also an arguer (an old-fashioned cooker).

Standing in front of the arguer is George Summer. He isn't a very tall person, probably around 5ft 6", with white skin, blue eyes, with brown hair. He is wearing silver-rimmed glasses, navy blue shorts, a cream short-sleeved shirt, and grey slippers. George is baking fresh bread, and at the same time cooking the children's breakfast. The smell of the bread baking fills the downstairs of the cottage and rises to the children's rooms.

The smell drifts into the girl's room where Scarlett and Abigail were laid in their bunk beds, Scarlett being laid on the bottom bunk, and Abigail lying on the top bunk. Scarlett is four years old, with white skin, blue eyes, and shoulder-length mousy brown hair. Abigail is seven years old, with white skin, silver eyes with shoulder-length dark brown hair.

The sun's rays are peeping through the girl's bedroom window, and onto the pillow where Scarlet's head rests.

Disturbed by the sun's rays on her face, Scarlet moves and stretches. She then gets a whiff of bread baking. Smelling this, she sits up suddenly, with a huge smile on her face, knowing her father is baking fresh bread, which she loves so very much, especially when it is cut straight from the oven. Freshly baked bread with melted butter is Scarlet's favorite.

"Abi, Abi, wake up (Abi being short for Abigail), Dad is baking fresh bread again" Said Scarlet to her sister. "Scarlet Let me sleep, I'm so tired," said Abigail. Scarlet then jumps out of her bed wearing her red check-pattered pajamas and clatters up the ladder of the bunk beds. She perches her head onto Abigail's mattress and says " Abi, but, but, dad is baking fresh bread, you know it's the best. "Leave me to sleep," said Abigail. And with that, Scarlet jumps down with a thud, pounces at the curtains, and pulls them wide open to the dislike of her sister. Scarlet runs out of the room to wake up her brother and tell him the news. She bursts through his bedroom door and almost trips over Elliot and his toys. Elliot is sitting on a multicolored rug in the middle of his room, with his toys forming a circle. Elliot is eight years old and has white skin, short brown hair, with brown eyes.

"Elliot what are you doing" asked Scarlet. "I'm having a tea party with my friends" replied Elliot. His friends were a grey, scruffy-looking toy dog, a brown bear covered with patches and one eye missing, an unusual-looking green and blue toy zebra, and a toy puffin.

"Elliot, Dad is baking bread again" exclaimed Scarlett. "I don't care, leave me alone said Elliot, and looked away with a frown. Scarlet, being upset by this walked out of his room, and went downstairs into the kitchen. "Dad, Elliot doesn't love me anymore," said Scarlet. " What gives you that idea" asked her dad. "Elliot told me to leave him alone," Said Scarlet. " well I know Elliot loves you, he's just upset at the moment because he has to go to the dentist tomorrow. Elliot fears the dentist. Here, take some bread" said Scarlet's father. George takes a loaf that he has just baked, slices it, and spreads butter onto it. The butter melts immediately. You can see the warm vapor rising from it. George then hands it to Scarlet on a white plate made out of bone China.

Scarlet's mouth rose sharply at the sides into the biggest smile she could make, and said "Thanks Dad, you're the best". and with that, the bread disappears into her mouth. After licking the last of the crumbs from her face, Scarlet says "Thanks Dad I love you", and then Wraps her arms around her dad. Her dad picks her up, swings her around, and tells her, " I love you too", before placing her down on the floor.

Meanwhile, Abigail was just getting out of bed. She looked a little unsettled after being woken by Scarlett. After stretching her arms out Abigail heads downstairs to the kitchen. "Morning Abi," said

George. "Morning Dad, breakfast smells nice," said Abigail. "You two go sit down for a while I serve up your breakfast" said George, he dishes up the girl's breakfast, bacon, sausage, egg, beans, tomatoes, and toast. The breakfast looked delicious.

The girls were just finishing their breakfast when Elliot walked into the kitchen. "Morning Elliot, you are looking a little grumpy this morning," Said George. "So" replied Elliot. "well you can be grumpy all you want too, but you are still going to the dentist tomorrow, whether you like it or not! and after you have had your breakfast, go and fetch the fresh eggs from the chicken coup" said George to Elliot. "girls go brush your teeth and get yourselves dressed, your clothes have been ironed, and are on my bed ready for you" Said Dad.

Elliot soon finished his breakfast and headed out to the chicken coup to fetch the eggs, leaving his Dad behind to wash up.

Out in the garden, Elliot was inside the chicken coup, letting the chickens out to walk around the garden. As soon as the last one was out, Elliot was acting like a little cheeky fox, gathering up all the fresh eggs. and once all the eggs were picked up, Elliot left the coup and locked its door behind him. Having just spun around from locking the door, Elliot caught a glimpse of his tree house in the garden. It is his prized possession. Elliot sat down on a stool his dad made and sat there looking at the tree house his dad had built for him. Looking at the treehouse, Elliot remembers the fun that they had together whilst making it and the fun that Elliot has had in it since. Thinking about it made Elliot feel guilty about being grumpy, and upsetting his sister Scarlet earlier when he told her to leave him alone.

Elliot returned to the house, finding his Dad sitting in his favorite place, reading the early morning paper that the paper boy had just posted through the door. "Sorry Dad, I didn't mean to be horrible," said Elliot, and hugged his dad. " That's OK, you should know though that the dentist isn't that scary. I went when I was a child. Besides it's Scarlet that you should be apologizing to," said George. With that Elliot runs upstairs and into the girl's room. Elliot Apologizes, "Sorry Scarlet, I shouldn't have said that to you". "That's ok, think I would be scared of the dentist too", said Scarlet. With that Elliot breaks a small smile and heads to his bedroom to get dressed.

The rest of the day passed very quickly. Elliot spent most of his time between playing with his toys in his room and riding his go-kart up and down the lane in front of the house. The girls spent most of their time dressing up and practicing for the school play in which they were appearing. George their father spent most of his time cleaning the house and washing the children's clothes.

A few hours later during the evening, George was out preparing a bonfire when Scarlet came running out into the garden. "Hi Dad," said Scarlet. "Hello, my little princess. Will you let your brother and sister know that in ten minutes I will be lighting a bonfire! And let them know I'm going to make some hot chocolate, and that we will toast some marshmallows together" Said George. With that Scarlet goes running back into the house to tell her brother and sister. George lit the fire and headed back to the house to make hot chocolate for everyone, and he got the marshmallows out ready.

Whilst George was getting the chocolate ready, the children stood waiting near the back door. The children knew that they were not allowed near the fire on their own, as it could be dangerous, so they waited sensibly for their dad at the back door. A minute later George opened the door, said, "Here you are", and handed the children a mug of hot chocolate each, and then they all headed to the fire together, George with a mug of hot chocolate in one hand, and a bag of marshmallows in the other. Once they reached the fire, they all sat down on some chopped-up logs that circled the fire and drank their hot chocolate.

The kids, especially Elliot had a chocolate moustache from drinking the hot chocolate. With the mugs empty, they placed them on the ground. George then handed the kids a hand full of vegetarian marshmallows each, and some sticks to put the marshmallows on so that they could toast them over the fire. "Remember children, don't leave them above the fire for too long, and let them cool a little before you eat them", said Dad. The children giggled upon hearing this, as on a previous occasion their dad had forgotten to let his marshmallow cool, and burnt his tongue when he placed it into his mouth.

The children toasted their marshmallows, one after the other, and ate them until they were all gone.

After sitting by the fire for ten minutes watching the fire burn, and enjoying the heat, George began to tell the children a ghost story.

The children were listening intensely, and at points throughout, were gripping each other with excitement and suspense. Although it was a ghost story, it was not that scary for children.

The children were all happy, and enjoying their time by the fire with their dad.

Time passed quickly, and it was getting late in the evening. The children by this point were feeling very tired and were beginning to yawn. George noticed that the kids were sleepy, so he decided it was time to get the children to bed. "c'mon you three, I think it's time for you all to get a shower and go to bed. "OK Dad," said Abi. "Really enjoyed tonight. love you Dad," said Elliot. George smiled. And with that, they all stood up and walked back to the house, leaving the fire to smolder away. The children, one by one headed upstairs, with George not too far behind. "go and tidy your rooms while I get the shower on" said George. The children went to their bedrooms to tidy up. George switched the shower on and called the kids one at a time to have their shower. The shower was brass in appearance and, above a traditional cast iron bath.

After drying the kids, George tucked each one of them into bed. The first to be tucked in was Scarlett. George pulled the covers up and kissed her on the forehead. Scarlet said, " What should I dream of tonight". with that, George answered, " Dream that you're a princess, that lives in a castle, on top of the clouds". next George tucked Abigail into bed. "What should I dream of Dad", said Abigail. "why don't you dream that you're on holiday, playing on a beach, and swimming in the sea", said George. He then places a kiss on top of Abigail's forehead and leaves the girl's room, turning out the light, and shutting the door behind him. "I hope you're in bed," said George, as he walked into Elliot's room. Elliot was just getting into bed. George leaned over Elliot and pulled up the sheets. "Love you Dad," said Elliot. "Love you too", said George, and he kissed Elliot on the forehead, before heading out of the room, turning off the light, and closing the door behind him. Elliot lay there looking out of his window for a while into the moonlight. It wasn't long before his eyes started to get heavy, and he began to fall in and out of sleep. Eventually, his eyes closed completely, and he fell fast asleep.

After sleeping Elliot felt refreshed. However, after pulling the blankets down from over his head, he felt not only refreshed but in a state of confusion. When Elliot pulled down the covers, he could see that his room was still dark except for the moonlight beaming through his window. This confused Elliot as he thought it was morning. What Elliot didn't realize is that he had indeed slept through the night until morning. after looking around he seemed more confused, for everything he looked at was shades of black and white. He sat up for a moment and scratched his head. Then came a worrying feeling, he then thought "What is going on." Elliot started to feel slightly scared, so he put on his dressing gown and slippers and headed to his Dad's bedroom. Upon entering the landing Elliot began to feel more scared, for all he could see was more shades of black and white, there was no other color, it had all gone. "Am I dreaming?" Elliot thought to himself.

Elliot then entered his dad's bedroom. His Dad's room was black and white also, the bed, bedding, walls, floor, and ceiling, everything was shades of black and white. After looking around the room, Elliot runs to the edge of his dad's bed. "Dad, Dad" Eliot cried, repeatedly. But no answer came. Eliot looked at his dad, he was sleeping. Eliot shook his dad, repeatedly saying, "Dad, Dad, wake up." but no answer came, nor did his dad wake. He tried to wake him, but no matter how hard he tried, he could not wake his dad. By now, Elliot had been trying for almost an hour. Elliot sat back, and tears began to fall from his eyes. After five minutes, Elliot wiped away the tears, and the thought of his sisters came to his mind. "They will help me Elliot thought. So, Elliot went to his sister's room. Their room was also black and white. He climbed onto Scarlet's bed. "Wake up Scarlet I need you," Elliot said. But no answer came. Elliot then climbed up to Abigail's bed. "Wake up Abigail, please wake up, I'm scared," said Elliot. Repeatedly, Elliot pleaded with his sisters, "Please wake up". he spoke. But no answer came. Elliot laid by his sister Scarlet wrapped his arms around her, and lay there, holding her close, crying.

After an hour, Elliot got down from Scarlet's bed and headed on to the landing.

Elliot looked into his Dad's bedroom, but his dad was still asleep. "What am I going to do?" Elliot said to himself. Elliot then thought, "Maybe I should look downstairs." So he went downstairs, and everything was the same, all black and white. All that was happening made Elliot feel lonely, so he walked into the kitchen and poured himself a glass of milk. This is what Elliot's dad does for him when he wakes up from nightmares and when he feels lonely. But this time Elliot's dad was not there. The difference is that Elliot felt he was still having a nightmare. Elliot wrapped his dressing gown around him as tight as he could, to both comfort himself, and give himself a feeling of security. He looked at the fire for warmth, but the fire was not alight. Elliot stepped back into the corner and slid down the wall. He just sat there, not moving, just looking, everything was still. Even the clock on the side, the hands, they were frozen, as if time was standing still.

All of a sudden there was a faint sound in the distance. "What was that" Elliot thought, "I'm sure I heard someone talking". he sat up, then jumped up. Listening. Where were the voices coming from? They sounded distant. As if they were coming from the garden. He climbed up onto the sofa and looked through the window. He could see something in the distance, at the bottom of the garden. Whatever it was, it was getting closer. For a moment Elliot felt relieved, but then unsure. He did not know what it was, or who it was. if it was anyone at all. But the more he looked, the closer it got, and the louder it became. "Voices, definitely voices, it has to be" Elliot thought. It got closer, and closer still. "It is someone," Elliot thought. By now, Elliot could see the outline of a body walking, then two bodies, three, four. "Perhaps they are here to help" thought Elliot. He ran to the back door, thinking that whoever it was could help. As the strangers got closer, Elliot felt unsure, so he tucked himself behind the door and peeped outside. Then they became so close he could see who it was. It was his toys, his favorite toys, they were walking, talking, and flying. Elliot could not believe it. He rubbed his eyes. Then looked again. It was still his toys, walking, talking, flying. And heading right towards him. The toys looked up and saw that Elliot was there. His brown bear pointed at him. The other toys stood still and looked for a moment. Then they all waved slowly at him. Elliot gasped, then went into a moment of shock and had the sudden feeling again of being scared. Elliot ran upstairs to his room. Poor Elliot, this was not the morning he expected. And he certainly had gone through the emotions in the past few hours.

After running into his bedroom, Elliot shut himself inside his wardrobe and pulled his dressing gown over his head. "It's not real, it's not real," Elliot said to himself. Then Elliot pulled down the gown from his head, and thought to himself, "It can't be real". He then peeped out of the gap in the wardrobe. He couldn't see anything, well anything that wasn't ordinary, apart from everything being black and white. Then he heard something. The voices, he could hear the voices again. He moved back as far as he could, still peeping through the gap in the door. Then all of a sudden, his toys were walking into his bedroom, apart from his toy bird who flew into his room, landing on his bookshelf.

Elliot by now could hear what the toys were saying. They were saying "Elliot, don't be afraid, we're here to help. We are your friends." Elliot did not know what to think. Everything was not normal, black and white, not being able to wake his sisters or dad, and now his toys talking to him. Again his toys spoke, " Elliot we are your friends, we won't hurt you, we're here to help, please Elliot, don't be afraid". Elliot's teddy bear, the one with the patches opened the wardrobe door slowly. "see Elliot, it is us, your toys" said his toys. Elliot lowered his arms and looked a little more relaxed now. "we are here to help Elliot", said Elliot's toys. "why won't my family wake up, and why is everything black and white, and why are you talking", asked Elliot. "It is because of the evil dentist", said the toys. "An evil dentist, why?", said Elliot.

The toys went on to tell Elliot,

"The evil dentist is trying to take control of all the toys in the world and trap them in our world. See we have a world of our own. When the children in your world go to sleep, we return by magic to our world, and when the children wake, we return by magic to your world, so that the children can play with all the toys. And by keeping all you children and adults asleep, we won't be able to return to your world. Thus keeping us trapped in our world, putting us at the mercy of the evil dentist. The thing is, our world lives because of magic. The magic comes from the imaginative play and joy children have from playing with all the toys. So after a while, if the children are not playing, magic will no longer be created, thus our world will eventually disappear, and all the toys with it.

The dentist though, does not see this, or believe it. He only cares for himself. The dentist needs to be stopped.

Where we live, our world is vast, and across the ocean, there is an island, this is where the dentist lives.

The dentist gets the magic for his spells, from rotten teeth he pulls out of children, and adults alike. He is planning on infecting all the children's teeth in your world so that he can come here and pull them all out. And turn the rotten teeth into magic, to keep all the children and adults in a deep sleep forever.

We call him the evil dentist because, unlike normal dentists who help people, the evil dentist infects healthy teeth so that he can pull them out and use them for evil magic spells. At the moment the dentist can't travel to your world, as the magic travel gateway is being protected by toys, preventing him from travelling to your world. But we are getting weaker, as he infects more and more of our world, he is sending more and more toys into a deep sleep. If we can't stop him, all the children, and adults in your world will never wake up, and the toys will never live, or feel the love of a child's play again.

After listening to the toys, Elliot began to wonder why if everyone was asleep, then why was he awake. So Elliot asked the toys, "Why am I awake then". the toys answered, " You were asleep like everyone else, but we woke you". "How," said Elliot. "With magic," said the toys. The toys then explained further, "We have a very wise old wizard called Pippin the magical, who used the last of his magic to wake you up and to send us here to your world so that we can take you back to our world so you could help. Pipin is the last of his kind. His magic comes from the imaginative play of children. And with all the children, apart from yourself being fast asleep, there is no magic left for him to use. He used the last of his magic to wake you. "But, why me?, I don't know how to stop the dentist!" said Elliot. Well' Pipin can see things, and what he told us, is that a child who believes in their imagination will beat the dentist". "Why me then," said Elliot. There are many children who use their imagination, but none of them uses it as often as you", remember yesterday morning when you sat us all in a circle on your rug, having a pretend tea party". "yes" said Elliot. "Imagination like that is what will beat the dentist" said the toys.

"I don't think I can do it," said Elliot. "You have to, If you don't your family will never wake, and eventually, you will fall back to sleep. you need to face your fear and beat the dentist," said the toys. Elliot thought about it. "I want my family to wake up, I don't want to be without them," said Elliot. "Then you must come with us" said the toys. Elliot sat down and thought about it. It was hard for Elliot because he was really scared of Dentists. "OK, I'll do it," said Elliot, in a shaky, nervous voice.

"What are your names?" said Elliot. "the toy dog said "My name is Henry". The brown bear said, "I'm Patch". The zebra said "I I am Rolie." The puffin said, "I'm Ginger." "But that is what I called you," said Elliot. "yes, that's right, we take the names given to us, by the children we belong", said Henry.

"So what do we do now," said Elliot. "we travel to our world by the magic tunnel," said Rolie. "But first we must get to the tunnel," said Henry. "yes, and that won't be easy, for although the dentist cannot travel to this world yet, he has the help of crows," said Rolie. The evil Dentist placed the crows into a deep sleep also, all except their leader, (King black), king black was twice the size of a normal crow, and he was as black as can be. The evil Dentist threatened to place king black in a deep sleep unless he stopped us. After agreeing to help the dentist, the dentist awoke King Black's army of crows so that he could hunt us down and prevent us from returning to our world. "So how did he know about us then," said Elliot. "The Evil Dentist has many evil worshipers who will do anything at his every demand, and of those are the Grongels", said Henry. Grongels are what used to be toys until they were smashed up by naughty children and pieced back together out of different parts. Because of this, the toys (Grongels), are now monsters, confused and tainted by the naughty children who recreated them" said Ginger. "one of the Grongels was seen flying away from a secret meeting we had with

Pipin the magical about waking you up to help us fight the Evil Dentist", said patch. "after seeing the Grongel leave the meeting, we had him followed, that is how we learnt of the crows, and their leader King Black. And should King Black succeed, he has been promised your world", said patch. "King Black agreed to do the deed. Therefore, the evil dentist reawakened his army of crows" said Rolie. Upon hearing this, Elliot did not feel comfortable, for the second thing that he is scared of the most is crows. It was like the dentist knew exactly what Elliot was scared of. Scary, shifty, dark crows, with awful sounds, not to be trusted. Elliot thought to himself, "Well I haven't seen crows near my house for over a year, it can't be that hard". What Elliot didn't know is that King Black and his crows were already on their way to stop Elliot and his friends from reaching the magic tunnel.

"Just so you know Elliot, the evil dentist knows your fears, he will bring to life all that you are afraid of. This made Elliot feel more scared, and yet more determined to defeat the dentist, as thoughts of his two sisters living endless nightmares whilst they are asleep, made him feel very sad. He does not want his sisters to suffer the fate of an endless nightmare.

"We should leave now, we don't know how long the magic will last that keeps the tunnel open", said patch. "that's right, we must hurry," said Ginger. With that, Elliot stood up and said "Let's go". they all walked down the stairs, apart from Ginger who flew. They were just about to go out the back door when Elliot spoke out, "Wait, I must get something". with that Elliot ran into the living room, grabbed his brown satchel, and headed to the kitchen. He opened the cupboard door, and pulled out the biscuit tin. He opened the lid, emptied the cookies from the tin into his satchel, and filled his aluminum water bottle with water. Elliot thought that it may be a long journey, and he might need food and water for such a long journey. Elliot then ran back upstairs, and returned with a torch, placing it into his satchel with the cookies and water bottle. Thinking that it will come in useful if it gets any darker. "Right let's go," said Elliot. So, with that, they all walked out the door, and into the back garden, one by one. Elliot is the last. Once he was outside, he looked around. Everything was silent, and shades of black and white. The moon was out in a cloudless sky. So, although it was dark, you could still see very far in the dark, and see the outline, and more of what was around. It was very eerie. Even the chickens in the coup were asleep. Patch whispered to the others, "We must be quiet, and move fast". with Rolie leading the way, they ran, dodging in and out of the apple trees, and ducking under the branches, they eventually made it to the bottom of the garden. "Bang, clatter", Henry had tripped over a pile of wooden boxes, making a right noise. "I hope no one heard us", said patch. "but everyone's asleep, how could they", said Elliot. "the crows, I hope the crows did not hear us", said patch. "Oh," said Elliot. "We must be extremely quiet," said Ginger. Elliot was looking up at the tall oak trees, which stood at the foot of his garden. "this is the furthest I have been for a long time since the great fire", whispered Elliot. For beyond the oak trees, lay a great forest, that earlier in the year, had caught fire. The fire almost spread to Elliot's house. Elliot and his sisters were told by their dad not to venture past here as the trees are severely damaged and could fall at any time. "It's time to go now Elliot", said patch. "But How far do we have to go", whispered Elliot. Patch replied, " To the abandoned village in the middle of the forest".

Elliot and his friends started their journey towards the abandoned village. They passed through the oak trees taking one step at a time into the burnt forest. Leaving home, and the cover of the oak trees behind. As they progressed further the extent of the fire damage could be seen, from the bushes on the ground to the tops of the trees, it was all burnt. Everywhere resembled the color and texture of charcoal. And what was once grass was a blanket of soot. Elliot remembered the forest before the fire, all lush, green, and full of wild animals. Elliot could not imagine it any more different if he tried.

Out of the corner of his eye, Elliot noticed a small pathway, partially hidden from sight, by burnt debris, and soot.

Elliot pointed at the path and said, "Me and my dad used to walk down that path to the village to fetch our groceries." "Then that is the way we shall go", said Patch. And with that, the group changed direction and started to follow the path. As they walked they kicked up clouds of soot. The path went on for quit a distance. It diverted left and right and up and down with the hills. The group followed the path further and around a bend to the right. All of a sudden there was a loud crashing sound, and the earth shook beneath their feet. A giant of a tree had fallen to the ground, unable to support itself with its burnt trunk. "My Dad was right it is dangerous, let's hope a tree doesn't fall on top of us," said Elliot. Once around the bend, the burnt forest opened up into a clearing. It was strange to see, the clearing gave an almost identical appearance of being covered in snow. However, it was not snow that blanketed the ground, but Six inches of deep soot, covering the path out of all sight.

In the not-too-far distance, Elliot and his friends could see a valley, and towards the end of the valley, they could see the path again. Elliot and his friends headed down the valley towards the path. The sides of the valley appeared higher the further they went, the sides were steep, and in places, there were what looked like miniature landslides of rock and stone, and in places, it covered the path. After about half an hour Elliot and his friends came across a small river. The river in places was up to twelve meters wide and in other places as narrow as three meters. The path ran alongside the river for some distance, before coming to a halt. But this was not the end of the path for Elliot and his friends. They had just reached a crossing point. The path continued to the other side of the water. Both sides linked by steppingstones. The location is so picturesque. And the sound of the water flowing over the small stones in the stream sounds so tranquil. "I remember playing here with my sisters," said Elliot. "I remember too," said Patch. "yes that would be right, we had a teddy bear picnic that day," said Elliot. They crossed over the stepping stones, they were very slippery. Elliot nearly lost his footing, having regained his balance very quickly. (Had that been you or I, we would have probably fallen into the water). Fortunately for Elliot and his friends, they had crossed over to the other side without falling in. quite remarkable considering nothing of them got wet. The path followed the side of the river for about a mile. The path crossed over the river again, this time by the joining of a small iron bridge.

All of a sudden they could hear a noise in the distance. It stood out by a mile for everything else in the forest was silent. "Quick, run, it must be the crows" said Patch. "that way, around that corner," said Elliot. The group ran as fast as they could with Ginger flying behind. As they got around the corner the path and river continued onwards. "Up here," said Elliot. He began to climb up the side of the valley. The side was steep, and halfway up they passed under a stone arch. "Just a little bit further," said Elliot. As they climbed further, the others could see where Elliot was leading them. For what there was just short of the top of the valley was a small cave. "Quick, inside," said Elliot. They all raced inside as quickly as they could, just in the nick of time. The crows were now flying overhead, and the sheer number of crows blackened the moon out from the sky. And no sooner had the crows come, had gone just as quick. "Let's wait here for a while, to make sure they have gone" Said Ginger. "We need to be extremely careful, for the crows will search and search until they find us" said Patch. So, Elliot and his friends waited.

Two hours had passed since they saw the crow's fly overhead. "I think it's time we continued on our journey", said Rolie. "I think your right", replied Patch. And with that Elliot and his friends started to climb down the side of the valley in which they had climbed earlier. It was far harder to climb down than it was to climb up. The ground was loose, and there was not much to hold onto, apart from the odd tree as they descended further down. They were only halfway down when suddenly Patch slipped down to the bottom. He let out a yell, as he fell. "Are you alright" asked Elliot. "I'm okay, apart from having a sore bottom, and being covered in dirt" replied Patch.

It took a few minutes before the others made it down to the bottom, where Patch was resting.

"So which way now" asked Rolie. Elliot replied, "We have to continue along this river for another two miles, and then we follow a small lane that the path crosses over. Patch picked himself up off the floor, and the group continued on the journey. It seemed hours since they had left Elliot's cottage behind. "I feel tired," said Elliot. The others also felt tired. "In a few more miles we should stop, and get some sleep," said Patch.

The path and river changed direction to the right, before continuing straight again. All along the right-hand side of the valley, there were lots of dark little caves. You could not see inside them; they were pitch black inside. Some caves where as big as a house, whilst others were as small as a sink. The dark caves gave Elliot a chill when he looked at them. They did look very eerie though. There could be all sorts of creatures inside them. As they continued a little further, Elliot and his friends could see a small stone bridge, that crossed over the river. "This place is called Dove Dale" Said Elliot. "It must have been very beautiful before the fire" said Ginger". Elliot replied, "It was, this used to be a lush, green open meadow, with poppy's growing along the sides. And there used to be children playing here all the time, Having stick races, where they would drop sticks into the water from one side of the bridge, and see who's floated to the other side the quickest. I used to like coming here." Elliot and his friends crossed over the bridge and walked down the lane and onto the meadow. As they crossed the meadow, Elliot remembered the happy times, he had here having picnics with his family. At first, the thoughts of his family made him smile, but then remembering where they were, and that they wouldn't wake up, left him feeling very sad. Two tears drifted down Elliot's face. "don't cry Elliot, if it's about your family, we will wake them again, I promise" said Rolie. And with that Patch took hold of Elliot's hand.

They were now at the end of the meadow. And beyond there were burnt trees, on either side of the path. The path continued onwards, climbing upwards towards the top of the valley.

After about ten minutes they were standing at the top of the valley side, with the meadow behind. They had reached the top of another valley. the other side was just as high as they are now, but the valley is not very wide, there is a stream that flows through the middle of it.

Elliot for a moment had almost forgotten himself, for he was taking in the views of the burnt forest from a high until Rolie spoke out "Which way now, the path has stopped". Elliot then realized that the path hadn't stopped, it had indeed continued across the other side. Elliot spoke, "There used to be a bridge here. It must have burnt down during the fire. The path continues over the other side."

As they stood looking down the steep edge of the valley, there was a roaring sound. They turned around to see where it was coming from, but before they could run, an army of crows was swooping down at them. The crows were coming from all directions. Elliot and his friends fought as much as they could, throwing stones, and sticks. But that was not enough to stop the crows. They had lifted Rolie off the ground. There seemed hundreds of them, all clinging to Rolie with their claws, flapping their wings. Rolie was being taken away by the crows. Tears were falling from Rolie's eyes as he looked down at his friends. Elliot screamed out "Rolie, NO......). There was nothing Elliot and the remaining toys could do to stop Rolie being taken away.

The remainder of the crows were still trying to attack Elliot and his friends. Two of the crows tried to take Elliot's satchel away. As they lifted the satchel, the cookies that Elliot had put in their earlier fell out. They bounced and rolled down the valley. Elliot pulled his satchel back from the crows, and it fell by his side.

Patch being quick thinking grabbed two pieces of flint and sparked them together against some wood, it caught fire. Smoke rose from the burning wood which the crows did not like. This kept them away for a brief moment, but not for long, they were swooping down again. As the crows were about to attack, the ground on which Elliot and his friends stood, gave way. Sending Elliot and his friends tumbling down the side of the valley, apart from Ginger who was flying in the air. Elliot reached out to grab onto a root that was sticking out of the side of the valley, he was going too fast. As soon as he felt it in his grasp, it was gone The further they fell, the further they were leaving the crows behind in the distance. Ginger flew helplessly down the side of the valley, unable to help his friends as they tumbled. The side of the valley seemed to crumble as Elliot and his friends tumbled down, with stones, and boulders of dried mud following Elliot and his friends. It looked like a mini avalanche. Eventually, Elliot and his friends could fall no further, they had stopped at the bottom.

They were all dirty looking from all the ash and dirt they had got covered in from falling down the side of the valley. Elliot was crying, for he had grazed his knee from falling down the valley. "Get up move, there's a cave over there, we need to get in there fast before they come back," said Patch. They all got up and ran as quickly as they could, jumping across the stream and into the cave, with Ginger flying by their side as they went. Once inside they all paused for breath. The cave was dark, damp and almost silent apart from a constant drip, drip, drip, of water from the ceiling of the cave onto the floor. After gathering their selves, realization of losing one of their companions took hold. Disbelief came across the group. They looked as though their hearts had sunk a million miles. Elliot and his remaining friends were broken in appearance. "What are we going to do" said Elliot, in a very hurt, upset way. After five minutes Patch answered "We must go on, not give up, and hope we will be able to save Rolie soon". "but how?, when we don't know where Rolie is!, or even if he is still alive!", said Elliot. "he will be, but for how long I don't know. The evil dentist will want his teeth," said patch. "Then we should hurry up so that we can defeat the evil dentist, and save Rolie," said Elliot. "We must wait here for a moment until the crows leave", said Patch. "You are right, we can't go out while they are still there, if we do we could end up in the same fate as Rolie" said Ginger. So, they waited and waited, and waited. But they could still hear the crows. By now Elliot was becoming restless. And started to wander around the cave. Although he could not see much, he could feel a slight breeze. So, Elliot followed it into the corner of the cave.

Meanwhile perched on the top of the valley were the crows, with their leader King Black, said to the others in a deep, crackly voice, "We must split into two groups, the first carry that dumb excuse of a horse back to our leer and keep him prisoner, and the rest of us will wait here for the rest to come out of that cave, then we will take them too". So the crows split into two groups, one group carrying Rolie away, and the other group staying behind in wait of Elliot and his friends.

As Rolie was being carried away, his head was hung down in disbelief. He was after all helpless. There was nothing he could do, apart from wonder about the fate of his friends. Memories came across his mind of the happy times he had when Elliot used to play with him. As he remembered tears filled his eyes and streamed down his face. Rolie disappeared into the distance............

Back in the cave Elliot followed the breeze further and realized, the breeze was coming from a tunnel. "I think I have found another way out", whispered Elliot. "that's great, but we must be quiet", said Ginger. So, one by one they walked down the tunnel, unaware as to where the tunnel goes. Then it came to him, Elliot remembered that he had a torch. He reached inside his satchel. Pulled it out and switched it on. Now they could see where they were going. The torch was only small and being small meant it did not give off much light, but just enough to see a fair distance. As their eyes followed the light they could see the walls of the tunnel, but not the end, the walls seemed to go very far, more than what the light of the torch could travel. "we have no choice but to see where it goes" said Elliot. So they proceeded onwards, going deeper into the dark tunnel. The tunnel looked as though it had been carved. It was oval-shaped and had a slimy texture upon its surface, caused by the dampness and water dripping down from the ceiling. Every so often down the tunnel, they could hear the echoes of the crows behind, cackling. Even though they were heading into the unknown, they felt a sense of relief from leaving the crows behind. But then feel a sense of guilt, for having left behind one of their friends, who they may never see again. The tunnel did go on and on, but they continued, they had indeed been walking for about an hour. The only problem was that the torch was now losing its power, and Elliot did not have any spare batteries. Then the light went out altogether. There was a feeling within the group that they had lost already. But then Patch pointed out, "I can see light ahead." indeed, he saw light. For it was the smallest amount of light that there could be. This was promising to the group. It certainly lifted their spirits. Elliot had a sigh of relief. It was the smallest piece of light because it was so far away. But this was hope that they could still make it out, and if they could make it out, then maybe they could succeed, defeat the dentist, save Rolie, and save Elliot's Family. With this belief inside the group, they picked up their pace and started walking faster. Eventually, the light grew larger, and they were standing just at the end of the tunnel. Slowly patch peeked out of the tunnel to make sure that the crows were not there waiting for them. The outside was silent. "I don't think they are here, the crows that is," said patch. He decided that he should go out alone and leave the others inside, just while he took a look outside, just in case the crows were hiding. Patch looked and looked, behind trees, at the tops of trees, and behind rocks. But he could not see anything. So, he waved the rest of the group out. Out in the fresh air, they felt a little relieved to be out of the dark tunnel. Elliot and his friends had walked so far through the tunnel, that they had reached the next valley. It seemed as though their adventure was far from over, but at least they were a step closer to reaching the magic tunnel as the route they had just taken had been a shortcut to the village compared to the path in which they were going to follow. Having gathered their bearings, by looking at the moon, they soon found the direction in which they should go. But before heading further along on their journey, they stopped for a rest. After all, they had been walking for such a long time now.

Having now rested, Elliot and his friends got up to their feet. And started to walk towards the village. With Ginger flying above.

Meanwhile, back in the evil dentist's castle, the dentist was becoming restless. So, the dentist pulled out a wide gold plate and placed it on the floor. He started to put unusual things into it, from bats' liver, witch-hazel, bones, and many more such items, whilst singing an enchantment. Then all of a sudden something began to happen. The plate began to shake and glow. The fire then beamed upwards about six feet into the air. But this was not no ordinary fire. The fire was purple. Then an opening in the middle appeared. It was a looking portal. A way to see and communicate with the human world. On the other side of the looking portal was the leader of the crows. The dentist's face appeared suddenly in front of the crows. The leader of the crows fell back, having been startled by the sudden appearance of the evil dentist. "well, have you stopped them" said the evil dentist. "err, err, no, not yet", said the leader of the crow. "NOT YET!!!!!!!" screamed the evil dentist. "But, but, we have captured one of them, we have the one called Rolie", said the leader of the crows. "well, at least that's some good news, keep him prisoner, until I find the location of their magic tunnel. Then we will transport the prisoner to my castle so that I can infect his teeth, turn them rotten, and pull them out for my spells", said the evil dentist. "we have the rest trapped in a cave" said the leader of the crows. "So what are you waiting for, go get them, NOW!!!", shouted the Evil Dentist. And with that' the Evil Dentist disappeared in a flash of grey and purple smoke. "You heard him, get down there and get them", shouted King Black. His army of crows lifted off the ground like a swarm of locusts, the noise from their wings, and cackling voices was tremendously loud, and very scary, for if you saw that many crows, you certainly would run, and not look back. The crows flew down to the cave, with some flying inside. Those that did venture inside the cave could see it was empty, they flicked their heads side to side, but could not see anything. "they're not here, there not here", the crows said, almost in tandem with each other, repeating each other's words, until the news filtered back to King Black who screamed, "they're not there, go find them, fly everywhere, I mean everywhere and don't come back until you know where they are". the crows lifted off the ground and spread, flying in different directions across the forest.

About an hour after leaving the tunnel, Elliot and his friends came across a clearing. "This place used to be called Apple Meadow. There used to be a circle of apple trees surrounding this meadow. And the meadow used to be full of wildflowers, with lots of different colored butterflies. This place looks completely different since the fire", said Elliot.

"which way now to the village", said Ginger. " We can rejoin the path to the village beyond the meadow", replied Elliot. "If we have to go to the other side then we must travel fast, in case the crows are near. We can easily be seen in the open" said Patch. Elliot and his friends looked around to check to see if any crows were flying around before making their move across the burnt meadow. "it's time to go, the coast is clear" said Henry. With that, they all made their move and started to run with Ginger flying. The distance between the two sides of the meadow was far. They were halfway across the meadow when Elliot and his friends heard the flap of wings in the distance. The noise was getting closer. "We must move fast before they see us," said Patch. As they reached the shelter of the burnt trees on the other side, the crows were just approaching the edge of the meadow. "We must hide quickly," said Ginger. They looked around for somewhere to hide. Elliot spotted an oak tree. It had an opening in its side and was hollow. Elliot and his friends climbed inside. "We must wait here for the crows to pass," said patch. "I'm tired," said Elliot. "We should sleep here for the night then; it is late and we have been travelling all day. When we are rested we can continue our journey in the morning. And hopefully, by then the crows will have gone" said Ginger. Elliot laid down against the inside of the tree, resting his head upon his hands. His eyes closed quickly, and then he was soon fast asleep. Ginger looked at Elliot and said, "It must be hard for Elliot, having to face this, and be away from his family". Henry replied " Yes it must" and lay next to Elliot to give him some warmth while he slept. Patch spoke to Henry and Ginger "You too should get some sleep also, I will sit here awake and keep watch". Ginger cuddled up to Elliot as well, and both Ginger and Henry fell asleep.

Patch sitting awake by himself, looked up at the stars and began to wonder if they would make it, and break the spell so that Elliot could be reunited with his sisters and father again. Patch turned to Elliot, and whispered "I promise you, I will get you home to your family again".

Patch spent the whole night wide awake, keeping watch to protect the others, even though he was very tired, and needed as much sleep as the others.

He sat there, spending the whole night looking up at the stars. They were the only thing that seemed to show any sign of life. They twinkled, even though the rest of the world was trapped motionless, in darkness, staying in a state of night-time, not changing to daytime, even though time was still passing by.

Morning soon came. Elliot, Henry, and Ginger were waking from their sleep. Elliot being the first, with Henry, and Ginger being woken by Elliot's movements, as they had spent the night cuddled up to Elliot to keep him warm. Elliot yawned, sat up, and stretched his arms out. "morning Elliot" said Patch, in a soft welcoming voice. "Morning" replied Elliot, in a sleepy voice. Elliot and Henry stood up and stretched their legs, and Ginger stretched out his wings.

"What's for breakfast, I'm hungry," asked Elliot. "I don't have anything for you to eat" said Patch. "Where hungry too" said Scruff and Harper. "we will all eat when we get to our world" said Patch. "The abandoned village is not far now, we should be there in a few hours. We can then travel to your world and eat, I am starving" said Elliot. "Then let's hurry," said Henry. "We can rejoin the path ahead, just through those trees over there," said Elliot. With that, they all started walking through the clearing towards the path. After about five minutes of walking in and out of burnt trees, they arrived at the path.

Elliot and his friends walked along the path until eventually they were at the edge of the abandoned village. It was the first time since the fire that Elliot had been to the abandoned village, (or waterside as it used to be known). The village looked ruined, crumbled, all burnt, with half the walls collapsed. The church in the distance still stood high and mighty, apart from it having no roof or windows. The shops, and houses, were all roofless and windowless. The greenery had gone. The village used to win awards, for best kept village. It used to be pristine, with well-manicured lawns and hedges. People used to travel here from afar to sit by the stream that flowed through the center of the village. It used to be a wonderful place to visit. If you had seen the place before, you would find it hard to take in about what it has now become.

Elliot could not believe the difference. He looked shocked at the sight. "Well, we are nearly there now, seeing the church is a good sign", said patch. "so where is your magic tunnel" asked Elliot. "it's in the graveyard" replied Henry.

They walked through the village towards the graveyard. Along the way, they came across a stone bridge that crossed the stream which flowed through the center of the village. Elliot paused for a moment, remembering the time that he and his family had leaf races here. They all dropped leaves into the water at one side of the bridge and ran to the other side to see whose leaf was carried first by the stream to the other side. The thought of this made Elliot smile.

As soon as they stopped, they heard an awful sound in the distance. Having heard this sound before, they knew it was the crows. "We must run," said Henry. "We can hide in the basement of the church" said Elliot. They moved as fast as their legs, and wings could take them. The door to the basement had burnt away, but the stone stairs remained. Once inside they sat there quietly, to not let the crows know that they were there. Up above the crows had stopped, and were now resting on the walls of the church. Elliot whispered, "So where is the entrance to the magic tunnel", "It is at the back of the graveyard. At the foot of the hill between the roots of an old oak tree" replied Patch. The hill was steep. And at the foot of it was a wall about four feet tall. The oak tree patch spoke of grew out the side of the hill, and some of its roots hung over, and down the wall. From a distance, you would not know there was a tunnel unless you looked closely. the tunnel was indeed between the roots, but further back, hidden.

While they waited, Elliot walked around the basement admiring the gothic stone architecture. "my dad said that this church was beautiful, something that should preserved. I can see why now, the detail is amazing" said Elliot.

Waiting for the crows to move on seemed to take an eternity for Elliot and his friends, for they had been waiting in the basement for around three hours for the crows to move. Patch was becoming increasingly restless. "We need to move, we may not have much time left to save Rolie, our family and friends, and both our worlds. "but what can we do, the crows are still above," said Elliot. "We need to move. We cannot risk waiting any longer," replied patch. "Then we will have to move fast," said Henry. Henry climbed up the stairs and peeked outside. What he saw, was what looked like around two hundred crows, gathered around on top of the walls and trees. After seeing what he saw, he went back down the stairs and told the others.

With Elliot not knowing where the tunnel was exactly, they agreed that Patch would take the lead, followed by Elliot, then Henry, and then Ginger. They lined up one after the other at the top of the stairs, ready to go. " when I run, you all follow as quickly as you can" whispered Patch. They all nodded in agreement. Patch picked up a stone and launched as far as he could to distract the crows. And it certainly did that for when it hit the ground, every crow had fixed their eyes in the direction in which it had landed. As soon as it had,

Patch started to run, followed by the others. They were running in and out of the tombstones, and sometimes jumping over them, towards the back of the graveyard. The thrown stone gave them a head start, but it was not long before the crows noticed them and were flying down towards them. Patch had reached the roots and was climbing through them into the tunnel, the others were waiting outside. Patch was in the tunnel, next to climb inside was Elliot. It was taking time to get inside. They need to hurry for the crows are nearby. And with that, Elliot was inside. Now it was Henry's turn to climb in. Henry was just through the roots when there was a terrible cry. The crows had captured Ginger and were carrying him away. Elliot screamed out, "NO……….". but there was nothing that he could do.

Elliot, Henry, and Patch took a moment to gather their thoughts. It was hard for all of them. They had now lost two of their companions.

They could hear the crows outside, cackling, and saying "We now have two of you. And you three will soon be caught." this made Elliot, Henry, and Patch feel sad. "We must go on" said Henry. Elliot looked down; it seemed as though he had already given up. Patch could see how sad Elliot was and took hold of Elliot's hand. "It's time for us to go to our world now. Two more steps into the tunnel, and we will be magically transported to our world", said Patch.

The three of them stood side by side, holding onto each other. Patch held Elliot's left hand, whilst Elliot held onto Henry's collar. The three of them walked onwards, and three steps later, they were being magically transported to the world of the toys. As they were being transported, everywhere around them changed color. The dark walls of the tunnel had gone, replaced by ever-changing multicolored swirls, which spiraled to a point, like water disappearing down a plug hole, and then all of a sudden everything went dark. And then just as soon as it got dark, there was light, a light blue light. The light grew larger, as they got closer. All of a sudden they were feeling themselves sliding down a tunnel towards the blue light. There was a sudden smell of chocolate. *"I smell chocolate,"* said Elliot. As they got to the end of the tunnel, they fell out of a great big hole in the side of a giant mountain and landed splash down, into a chocolate lagoon. As Elliot looked back at the hole in the mountain he could see a giant chocolate waterfall, pouring out of the cave. It must have been around four meters high. There was chocolate everywhere.

Meanwhile, back in Elliot's world, the crows had just arrived back at their lair. King Black the leader of the crows was being spoken to, by the evil dentist. The crow noticed his army of crows heading back, with Ginger. "We have another" exclaimed King Black. With that the Evil dentist cast his gaze upon the oncoming crows, saying "Good, good, now where are the rest". in reply, one of the crows carrying Ginger said, " They disappeared inside a hole, and when we went to get them, there was no one there".

"that must be the magic tunnel, DAMN. Right, at least one thing we know where the tunnel is now. I want you to bring the two prisoners to me through the magic tunnel. Once you get to my side head south, and keep going south, in a few days, you will reach my land, and my castle. I will be waiting." King Black nodded, and said, "I will make sure they get to you". the evil dentist then disappeared in a puff of purple smoke.

King Black had not fulfilled his promise to the evil dentist of stopping Elliot and all his friends. And even though this was the case, he hoped that with having caught two of them, the Evil dentist might take mercy, and not send him and his crows to sleep.

King Black spoke out, "Get ready we leave in five minutes for the tunnel. And make sure the prisoners are tied up tight so they cannot get away". the crows tied up the prisoners, and got themselves ready. "Right, it's time to leave," said King Black. His army of crows took flight, with some of the crows holding onto Ginger and Rolie. They made their way to the tunnel.

Back in the world of toys, Elliot, Henry, and Patch were just stepping out of the chocolate lagoon and onto dry land. Although it was dry, it was not what you would expect in the world we know and live in.

The land looked like it was covered in grass. But it wasn't grass, it was thin strips of green sugar paper. Elliot couldn't believe what he was seeing, or what he just swam out of. Elliot licked his lips and said, "Chocolate, I knew it, chocolate". he could taste the chocolate that was covering his body and face. He could smell the sweet smell of chocolate. He ran back to the edge of the chocolate lagoon, dropped to his knee, and started to lick up the chocolate, as though he was a cat lapping up milk. For Patch and Henry, this was nothing new, this was their world. They were used to it, unlike Elliot, who looked like he had been given the keys to a sweet shop and allowed to eat anything he wanted. Patch and Henry were just as hungry as Elliot, for they had not eaten the previous day either. They started eating the sugar paper grass. Elliot turned around having just drunk the largest amount of chocolate he had ever had in his life, noticing Henry and Patch eating the grass. "Can you eat that too", asked Elliot. "Come and try it" replied Henry. Elliot took a large handful and shoved it into his mouth all at once. His eyes lit up. "Sugar paper", Elliot said with amazement. And as he did, bits of it flew out of his mouth as he spoke.

Their tummies were all now full, and the feeling of hunger had gone. Elliot and his friends sat down for five minutes, just to let their tummies settle before they continued on their journey. Whilst they were sat down, Elliot looked around in amazement. The world was full of color. Elliot noticed what looked like a tree, with colored balls on it. Elliot pointed at it and asked, "What is that". "That is a chocolate bubblegum tree. The tree trunk is chocolate, the leaves are made of green gummy sweets, and the balls are bubblegum," said Patch. "that's amazing," said Elliot. As Elliot looked further, he could see many flowers. What do they taste of, asked Elliot, pointing to the flowers. "The flowers here taste like fruit, banana, pear, apple, orange, strawberry" answered Henry. "that's amazing," said Elliot.

"We need to move now, Pipin the magical will be waiting for us," said Patch. Elliot and his two remaining friends stood up, and started walking. "it's this way," said Henry. They followed a stream of chocolate that flowed from the chocolate lagoon. It flowed downwards, through a valley. The valley sides were about ten meters high. And the sides were like layered rock built up over the years. But this was not rock. The layers here were layers of sponge and jam. As they walked along Elliot grabbed a piece of the valley side and started to eat it. After finishing his mouthful, Elliot said "Amazing. I cannot believe this is real." The chocolate stream flowed for about two miles, and as they went the valley sides got lower and lower. Until there were no sides at all. And the ground was almost flat, apart from the odd rolling hill. The whole land was covered in sugar paper grass. And every so often there was a chocolate bubblegum tree. As they walked closer they came across a group of toy pigs, they were pink and made of soft rubber. They were eating the bubblegum off the trees. Strangely as the pigs ate, every so often there were bubbles of bubble gum being blown out of their bottoms, which floated up to the sky. This made Elliot laugh. Toy pigs blowing bubbles of bubble gum out of their bottoms. Well, you got to admit, it is kind of funny.

Elliot and his friends walked on for a further ten minutes and came across a meadow. This meadow was full of wildflowers. Not like the wildflowers we know and smell. These flowers had hollow stems made from candy rock, and the flower heads were made of sugar, which tasted of all different kinds of flavors, from cola to cream soda. And there were also mushrooms, made of chocolate with marshmallow centers. As Elliot and his friends walked through the meadow, Elliot plucked and ate the odd sweet flower and chocolate mushroom. The smell from the meadow was like the smell you get when you walk into a sweet shop, but so much more intense. Eventually, they reached the end of the meadow and were now at the beginning of a great forest. The forest was full of giant trees made out of chocolate, with jelly leaves. These trees made Elliot and his friends look extremely small. As Elliot looked up at how tall the trees were, he noticed the sky was getting much darker, from a pale blue to a dark, deep blue. And without notice, the sky started to rain. As the rain ran down Elliot's face, Elliot licked his lips. The rain tasted of strawberries and cream. As they continued their walk, with Patch taking the lead, Elliot kept sticking his tongue out to catch the rain to drink it. After about five minutes the rain stopped.

Fortunately for Elliot, there was the odd bush scattered throughout the forest with upturned jelly leaves. The leaves had filled with the strawberry cream rain. Elliot pulled at one of the leaves and tipped the contents into his mouth.

Patch now, was starting to become a little impatient with Elliot constantly stopping. "Elliot, we need to hurry, remember what we are here to do," said Patch. "Sorry," said Elliot. He then started to walk faster. "How far do we have to go," said Elliot. "We will be at the tree village in about half a day. And to get to the Evil dentist's home, many more days" replied Henry. On their journey to the tree village, Elliot saw all kinds of toys. Elliot recognized the toys that his friends owned. As they walked further the land became very steep. This slowed their pace. And after a while the ground started to level out, and walking became easier for them. For Elliot, it seemed as though he had been walking for a day. The trees became less dense, and there was an opening. In the middle of the opening, there was a deep crack, about thirty meters deep, and four meters wide. Flowing through the crack was a river of strawberry milkshake. And bridging across the crack was a fallen tree. The tree was hollow. "We must cross here," said Patch. He then led the way, by walking into the hollow of the tree, to get to the other side. Elliot and Henry followed behind. The whole experience of this world seemed unreal for Elliot. He could not believe what he was doing. The fact that he was now walking through a chocolate tree, made him smile even more. Once they were out of the tree, Elliot looked back at what he had just done, snapped a piece off the tree and ate it. You would think that by now his tummy was full, but he continued to snack now and then.

"Where nearly there," said Patch. I guess the reason behind his saying, is because he could hear many voices in the distance. As they walked further the voices grew louder. And then right before them was the tree village. It was an array of tree houses, high above joined by walkways, made from the branches of chocolate trees, bound together with vines made from licorice. The village was extremely large, with about fifty tree houses. And in the middle of the village was a giant of a tree, with a spiral stairway, circling it going upwards to the village.

"This is where Pipin the magical lives," said, Patch.

Elliot and his friends made their way up the spiral staircase to the village. Elliot however was not too keen on heights, he held onto the vines which grew up the side of the tree tightly, so as not to fall. The tree was indeed tall. Eventually, they got to the top. The toys that lived in the village were waiting there for them. There was a small, chubby brown bear standing central ready to greet them. "Welcome. we have been expecting you. Pipin the magical would like to see you all", said the brown bear. He then led the way to the home of Pippin the magical. Cola bubbles were flowing out of the windows and doorway. As they got close, a voice spoke out "Come in". it was Pippin the Magical. Elliot and his friends walked inside. And what Elliot found was a small, and very old man, who had a long grey beard. He was wearing a dark cloak and hat. The hat had a thin rim, like a saucer, and was pointed in the middle. He was cooking something in a large cauldron. This was where the cola bubbles were flowing from. "Hello Elliot, I have been expecting you," said Pippin the Magical. "but, but, you're a man," said Elliot. "I guess you were expecting a toy," said Pippin. "Yes," said Elliot. "If you sit down, I will explain everything," said Pippin. Elliot, Scruff, and Patch sat down on the floor. Before speaking Pippin blew out the flame that was heating the cauldron.

Pippin' the magical went on to explain his story.

"An exceptionally long time ago my ancestors used to live in your world. They found themselves being pushed out from society, due to them having magical powers. For not being wanted in your world, my great, great, great, great, great grandfather created this world, out of the imagination and dreams of children. What he found was, when he created it, that for some reason or another the toys with which children played, were able to exist in this world when children slept in yours.

So for many years, the toys and my kind have lived together peacefully.

For this world to continue, children need to dream and play using their imagination. And as you know the children in your world are under a spell, keeping them asleep with nightmares instead of dreams. The spell needs to be broken for our sake, and the sake of the children. They shouldn't be kept prisoner in their sleep. To break the spell, you must defeat the Evil Dentist.

It is with a heavy heart, that I tell you this. The Evil Dentist is my younger brother. I would have stopped him myself, but I have no more magic left. I used my last waking you from your sleep. As my kind gets older, we lose our magic powers. And with my brother being much younger, he still has magical powers. We are the last of our kind, so there is no one else left with magic powers to defeat him. He can only be defeated by a child of great imagination. This is why I woke you up. You have the biggest imagination that I have ever known. What you need to do is believe, and you will defeat him. Besides having the gift of magic, I have another, that is being able to see into the future. I get glimpses of what will soon be. And what I saw was you celebrating defeating my brother, so I know you are the one".

"The one thing you do have on your side is a spell I placed whilst I still had some magic, this prevents my brother from leaving his castle. This is why he uses his evil henchmen to do his bidding" said Pippin the magical.

Just as the spell caster finished what he was saying a toy bird flew into the home of Pippin the magical. The bird was gasping for breath, trying to say something.

"settle down, take some deep breaths, then tell us what you want to say," said Pippin the magical. The bird sat down, and after a few minutes had got his breath back. The bird then explained, "I have just seen a dark cloud, head south. The dark cloud was a vast swarm of crows. And they were carrying two toys with them". This grabbed the attention of Elliot, Patch, and Henry. "It must be Rolie and Ginger. Their still alive," said Henry. "They must have come through the magic tunnel," said Patch. "they will be carrying your friends to my brother" said Pippin the magical. "we need to hurry" said Patch, with a worried look on his face. "You cannot leave yet. It will soon be dark. The forest is full of my brother's Grongels when it is dark. You may get caught. Sleep here in safety, then head out in the morning when it gets light", said Pippin the Magical. After listening to what the wizard said, Elliot and his friends thought it

was best to wait until morning. Pippin the Magical made up some
hammocks for Elliot, Henry, and Patch to sleep in. and also made
them something to eat. Elliot having eaten so much earlier
throughout the day, was very full, and he didn't eat very much.
Henry and Patch did not eat much either, for they were worried
about Rolie and Ginger. During the evening Elliot sat just outside of
the doorway. He was looking up at the stars, thinking about his dad
and sisters, and when they used to sit together looking up at the stars,
using their imagination to make pictures with them. Whilst Elliot sat
there, Pippin the Magical came and sat beside Elliot and started to
speak to him. "Elliot, the journey ahead will not be easy, and it is a
long way to my brother's castle. I am to old travel, so I have made
you a map. If you take a look you will see how far you have to go.
Once you leave the protection of the woodland realm, you have to
journey across ice cream mountains, Sail across bubble-gum sea,
Journey across jelly bear lands, and navigate through swamplands.
And finally, climb up the honeycomb mountains to the castle where
my brother lives. The journey will be long, and you will face many
enemies. My brother has an army of Grongels, they are the creation
of naughty children who took toys, broke them into pieces and
joined the different parts together to create monstrous, disfigured,
evil toys. As well he has also created monsters from the nightmares
and fears of children, many from your own. If I were you I would go
to bed, and rest as much as I can. Here put this map in your satchel".
Pippin hugged Elliot. And then Elliot stood up and went to bed. For
the next hour, Pippin the magical sat alone outside, thinking about

what his brother had become. This made him feel incredibly sad.

It was just about morning, and daylight was shining through the windows. All of a sudden, there was a loud noise outside. This woke Elliot, his friends and Pippin the magical. They could hear shouting. This made them all jump up quickly and run to the door. Once outside they could see what was happening. The tree village was under attack from the Grongels. There were toys already outside fighting against the Grongels. Elliot and his friends were soon part of the fight. Grongels were coming from all directions some were flying, whilst others were climbing the great stairway and filling the walkways. Elliot and his friends where being attacked by at least ten Grongels. Two of the Grongels had grabbed hold of Henry and where trying to fly away with him. Elliot reached out and pulled Henry back. The Grongels let go of Henry. The battle seemed to go on for ages. And at one point it looked as though the toys were losing the battle. Toys were being pushed from the walkways, and others were being carried away. The toys fort bravely. But there were many more Grongels than there were toys. Then all of a sudden there was a loud bang and crackle, it sounded very much like lightning. Toys and Grongels were both startled by this and all turned round to face where the noise had come from. The noise came from Pippin the Magical. He had slammed his old magic staff down on the floor. He then shouted out as loud as he could, "pull the Grongels apart, they are not made like you". this made sense as the Grongels had been pieced together by naughty children, who just shoved various toy parts together. The toys upon hearing what Pippin the Magical said, started to pull at the Grongels. Their arms, their legs, their heads, tails, and wings. They Grongels were being pulled apart by Elliot and his friends. And their parts where separating with very little effort. It was not long before the toys outnumbered the Grongels. The Grongels parts were being thrown onto the ground down below. And after a short while the parts were starting to build up into a large pile on the floor. The remaining Grongels started to retreat, running away, they knew they were beaten. "I don't think we will see them again," said Pippin the Magical. The toys had won. They were celebrating together, jumping up and down, and shouting Hooray. "Well done everyone," said Pippin the Magical. Elliot hugged Henry and Patch in celebration. "What will happen to the parts of toys that used to be Grongels" asked Elliot. "Once the dentist has been defeated, we will spend many weeks piecing together the parts into the toys they used to be, and bring them back to life" said Pippin the magical.

"That will be good" said Elliot". "yes, but we need to put our focus on saving our friends and family right now" said Patch. "yes, we should, we don't have much time, Rolie, and Ginger will soon be at the castle. I think you should take Defender, our toy knight, he can help you on the journey, he is extremely strong, and is built of the hardest material", said Pipin the magical. With that, Defender the Knight stepped forward. He was a very tall toy, almost as tall as Elliot. He had shiny silver armor, a shiny silver shield with a purple outline, and a very long sword. "I will help you. I miss being played with by my toy owner. I can't help but think of him being fast asleep, suffering horrible nightmares", said Defender. "your most welcome to join us" said Elliot.

"I wished I could have gone with you, but I am afraid that I am too old, and have no magic left" said Pippin the Magical. "We will be ok. And it looks like you will be needed here to help repair the tree house village, and in putting the Grongels back together to how they used to be", said Patch. "your right, but right now we need to prepare you for the journey ahead. On your journey, you will find that our world is not what it used to be. My brother the evil dentist has poisoned some of the land around his castle, and it is spreading outwards. If you eat anything you will fall fast asleep, under the same spell that he has placed everyone under in your world Elliot. So you must take some food to eat when you get there. I know you like cookies, so I have made you some in anticipation of your journey ahead. There is enough to fill your satchel, and also plenty of fresh water for you to bottle up and take", said the Pipin the magical to Elliot. "I have made you all some as well," said Pippin the Magical to Patch, Henry, and Defender. "Thank you, you are very kind", said Patch.

Pippin the Magical went to his home and returned with the food and water for everyone. "You must hurry. This battle has cost us enough time", said Pippin the Magical. And with that Elliot filled his satchel with food, and filled up his water bottle with water. "here I have three satchels for you three to carry food and water in", said Pipin the magical to Patch, Henry, and Defender. They each took a satchel, and filled them with food and water. "don't lose your map" said Pippin the Magical to Elliot. "I won't" replied Elliot. With that, they all made their way down the spiral staircase to the ground below. Once back on the ground, the tree houses looked so small.

They started back on their journey, making their way through the forest. As they walked through the trees, every so often, Elliot plucked the occasional flower from the ground and ate them. These resembled daffodils, and they tasted of lemon and smelled very sweet. The further they went away from the village, the quieter the forest was becoming, and also there were not as many toys around. "What happened to all the toys, the forest used to be full of them" said Patch. Defender replied, "Since you had been gone in the real world, toys have been vanishing, with the occasional sighting of Grongels disappearing in the distance. We believe the Grongels had been snatching the toys away to the evil dentist's castle". "it is horrible to think that someone could be so bad in doing all this" said Elliot.

Two hours back into their journey, the forest was starting to become less dense. And within twenty minutes they arrived at the edge of the forest.

They stood still for a moment, looking at the journey ahead. For in the distance were ice cream mountains, and between them and the mountains was a long open plain. To you or me, that is a stretch of flat land that seems to go on forever.

"It is a long walk to the mountains, it normally takes me half a day", said Defender to Elliot. "and we will be out in the open for all to see. Let's hope the evil Dentist has no one out trying to stop us on the plains. The plain is almost flat apart from the occasional rock, and the ground is made from different colored nougat. Elliot reached down and placed a piece of it into his mouth. The others looked and smiled. Elliot smiled back and said, "It tastes good". with that, the others laughed. Henry said, "Don't you stop eating", in a joking way. Elliot replied, "Sometimes", and smiled as he swallowed the last piece. They walked for a few hours then stopped, to drink some water, and to rest their legs for a brief moment. "well at least were over halfway there now", said Defender. The rest didn't last long, five minutes to be precise. They all stood up and continued with their journey. "what's that in the distance" said Henry. "I can't see anything", said Elliot. "I can," said Patch. "It looks like some Grongels are attacking a toy", said Defender. "let's go," said Patch. And with that, they all started to run towards the Grongels. As they got closer they could see three Grongels attacking a toy hedgehog. As they got to within a few meters, Defender pulled out his sword and started to strike out at the three Grongels. As he hit them with his sword, the Grongels body parts, were separated into pieces. And before the others could do anything, the Grongels were just a pile of toy parts on the floor, lifeless. "are you ok", said Elliot to the hedgehog. "I am now. They were trying to take me away to the evil dentist's castle, but were struggling to carry me because of my spikes", said the Hedgehog. Eliot and his friends introduced themselves. My name is Elliot, they call me Patch, my name is Henry, and I am called Defender. The hedgehog replied, "They call me Cuddles", and asked "Where are you going". "where on our way to defeat the dentist, "said Elliot". "Can I join you" asked Cuddles. "yes, you may be able to help us", replied Elliot.

With that, they all continued on their journey, with the company of a new friend.

After walking for about an hour with their new companion (Cuddles), they had reached the end of the plain and were standing at the foot of ice cream mountains. The mountains were not like they were back in the real world, they were much bigger, and not to mention, made of ice cream. Elliot could see all different flavors, strawberry, rum and raisin, banana, chocolate, rocky road, vanilla,. There was pretty much every flavor of ice cream you could imagine. And now and then, there were wafers sticking out from the mounds of ice cream, scattered everywhere. Looking both left and right, the mountains seem to go on for miles. And you've guessed it, Elliot is trying the ice cream. "this place is amazing", said Elliot. "come on Elliot, we need to move, you will have time to eat as much as you want on the way back", said Patch. They all looked up at the task ahead of them. "it is high, isn't it", said Elliot. "yep, but we need to get climbing", said Patch. Patch stepped forward, and started to climb the mountain. The others quickly followed. With almost every step, they were slipping, struggling to stay on their feet. Elliot was thinking to himself, "This is the hardest bit of the journey yet, I hope it gets easier after this. The pace was slow going. And after about thirty minutes they had made little progress, when all of a sudden, Patch slipped. As he slid back, he tumbled into Defender, who tumbled into Henry, who tumbled into Elliot, who tumbled into Cuddles. And in no time at all, they were all back at the bottom of the mountain. "We're never going to climb this mountain", said Patch. "but it was great fun though", said Defender. "I have an idea," said Elliot. And with that, he picked up some broken wafers, and licorice laces from the floor, and began to tie the wafer to the bottom of his shoes with the laces. He then began to climb up the ice cream mountains, this time by climbing up the valleys, where the mounds of ice cream join. As he climbed with every step, he drove his shoes with wafers attached into the sides of the valley. This was a great idea, his feet did not slip. After seeing how well Elliot was climbing, the others tied wafers to their feet and started to climb behind Elliot. "wait, grab a load of those licorice laces, we might need it for rope later", said Elliot. Defender picked up some lace tied the pieces into a rope, and swung it over his shoulder, he then followed the others up the mountain.

After four long hours, they were nearing the top, their climb had been slow, but at least they were nearly there.

As they stepped closer, the ice cream started to disappear beneath their feet, hidden by strawberry syrup, which coated the tops of the mountains, along with sugar-coated cherries of all sizes, from the size of footballs right up to the size of a large van. As Elliot stepped onto the syrup, the wafers tied to his feet began to dissolve immediately, and he found himself slipping slowly backwards. Elliot spoke out, "We need to change our plan or we will all slip back down the mountain. Let's make a human ladder, we are only ten feet from the top. Defender stuck his feet deep into the mountain, and the others climbed on top of one and another's shoulders. Elliot being the last to climb took the licorice rope from Defender and made his way to the top of the ladder. Although the ladder was long they were still short of reaching the top. Elliot tied a loop with the end of the licorice rope and threw it over the top of one of the cherries that was stuck into the top of the mountain. He tugged at the rope to see how strong it was, but the cherry did not move. So, he climbed up the rest of the way by pulling himself up with the licorice rope. Once at the top he sat down and waited for the others.

After seeing Elliot climb up the rope, cuddles soon realized he and Henry could not climb up with the rope, as they did not have any hands. Cuddles shouted out, "Wait a minute, me and Henry can't climb the rope, we have no hands". "I have an idea", said Defender". and with that, he tied the bottom of the rope around Cuddles, and told Henry to hold the rope with his teeth. "me, Patch, and Elliot, will pull you both up. With that, he and Patch made their way to the top. Once there, all three then pulled Cuddles and Henry up to the top. It wasn't very easy to pull the two of them up, but Defender was incredibly strong. Once they were both at the top, Defender undid Cuddles from the rope. "thank you", said both Cuddles and Henry. Just as they had made it to the top, darkness was beginning to set over the land, and the sun was setting in the distance. "we must find somewhere to rest for the night", said Patch. "we can use that giant cherry over there", replied Defender. They all walked over to the giant cherry. "How can we use this?" asked Elliot. "Watch," said Defender. And with that he took his sword from his back, thrust it deep into the heart of the cherry and then carved out the center of the cherry. "It looks like an igloo", said Elliot. "we can all sleep in here", said Defender. "that was a really good idea", said Patch. They all stepped inside the cherry. It was much warmer inside the cherry than outside of the cherry on the ice cream. "I am very tired", said Cuddles. "me too", said both Henry and Defender. The three of them cuddled up together at the far side of the cherry, and in no time they were all fast asleep, except for Elliot and Patch. "I can't sleep, I can't help but worry about Ginger and Rolie", said Elliot. "I know, I understand, I worry about them too", replied Patch. "come here and sit with me", said Patch. Elliot sat down with Patch at the entrance of the cherry. Patch placed his arm around Elliot. And they both sat there looking out into the night sky.

As they both sat there, the sky got darker and darker as time went by. In the distance, where the sun set, the sky was beginning to glow, there were beams of light stretching out all over the sky, moving as if they were waves. The beams of light changed color. It was amazing. As Elliot and Patch sat there, they watched the colors change in the sky. "It reminds me of the northern lights. My dad took me to see it once in Scotland", said Elliot. "I find it very relaxing", said Patch. They must have sat there watching it together for at least two hours, until Elliot fell asleep, with his head resting on the side of the entrance of the cherry. When Patch noticed Elliot had fallen asleep, he picked him up and laid him next to the others. And then laid down alongside to keep Elliot warm, and then he fell fast asleep.

It was the next day when the sun started to shine through the opening of the cherry. Beams of light shone onto Elliot's face, and this woke him from his sleep. "Wake up, wake up everyone, it's morning already", said Elliot. Hearing Elliot's voice, the others woke from their sleep. "Morning everyone", said Elliot. "Morning," replied the others. Elliot stepped outside of the cherry, followed by the others. Elliot paused for a moment to take in the view. He could see the forest in the distance, where the spell castor lived. It was so far away, it looked very small.

 Looking the other way, Elliot could see the bubblegum sea, it stretched out far into the distance. And at the foot of Ice Cream Mountain, he could see Pirate Cove. Patch spoke, "That is where we need to be, down there, we can catch a boat ride to sail across the sea". "Yes we can, but we must first have something to eat", replied Henry. They all sat down and ate some of the cookies that the spell castor had made for them from the previous day. As they were finishing their breakfast, snow began to fall from the sky, not the snow that you and I would know, this snow was tiny little specks of pink candy floss. This world is amazing, thought Elliot, as he watched the snow drift down. A few minutes later Elliot and his friends could hear what sounded like a stampede. They looked down at the path in which they had just climbed the previous day, and what they saw, worried them. There was a small army of icing soldiers. They were all white, with razor-sharp teeth, they almost resembled ghosts. "We need to move now, the ice men work for the evil dentist" said, Defender. And with that they all slid down the other side of the mountain, leaving the ice men behind.

As they slid down, they got faster and faster, sometimes getting thrown up into the air, from where ice cream stuck out from the side of the mountain, before landing back on their bums and sliding back down the mountain. They slid in and out of cherries, and underneath great arches made of wafer. The slide down was amazing. The longest slide in the world. They all cheered in excitement as they went. Five minutes later, they were already halfway down the mountain. The journey down was nowhere near as long as the journey up. Another five minutes later they were near the bottom of Ice Cream Mountain. They were going so fast, they did not stop there, they slid straight into the sea, with great big, splashes, and a giant cannonball, made by Defender, the spray went up almost twenty feet in the air. "That was amazing, but what about the ice men?" said Elliot. "They won't come down here, because of the sea, it will dissolve them", said Patch.

As Elliot stepped out of the sea, he paused to look around. The cove fascinated him. It reminded him of north landings at Flam borough head, a place he visited on holiday. The cove was like a natural harbor, it had a shape like two hands, almost cupped together in a curve, and at the end of one curve, there was a large tree, which resembled the shape of a hook. The was a small dock made out of chocolate fingers, with a small boat with two sails. At the foot of the dock was a small hut, that resembled that of a Tikki bar. And around the cove, was lots of small caves. The land surrounding was built up of layers of sponge and jam.

"We need to find the captain of that ship, to sail us across the sea", said Patch.

"he's probably in that hut" replied Henry. The group of friends entered the hut, and sitting in the corner was the captain. The captain did not resemble what you would expect a captain to be. The captain was a toy girl. She was not very tall, she wore a black hat that was tilted to the side, with a red feather. She had a white shirt, and blue shorts, with ragged edges. She was drinking pineapple juice out of the shell of a coconut. Patch spoke out, "Captain we need your help, we need to sail across the sea to jelly bear lands". "now why would you want to go there?", asked the captain. "where going to defeat the evil dentist" replied Elliot. "in that case, I will take you. And you can call me Rosa, captain Rosa", said the captain. "thank you" my name is Elliot, this is patch, Henry, Defender, and Cuddles", said Elliot. "nice to meet you all," said Rosa the captain. "nice to meet you all too", replied Elliot's friends. "well, are you all ready to set sail", said captain Rosa. "Yes," replied everyone. "Well, let's get going", said captain Rosa. They all made their way out of the hut, towards the ship, when all of a sudden there was a loud crash, followed by another, then another. They all turned around. It was the icing warriors, they were throwing ice balls at Elliot and his friends, from the side of the mountain. The ice balls rained down from the sky. "Run everyone," shouted Captain Rosa. Everyone ran as fast as they could. Having reached the ship, they were out of the reach of the ice balls. "Is everyone OK", said Captain Rosa. They all replied "Yes", then looked around at each other. "where's Henry", gasped Patch in fear. They looked around. He was not with them. They looked back towards the hut. Scruff was stud still, frozen to the spot. One of the ice balls hit him and froze him solid. Elliot could not take any more, he burst out crying. Patch wrapped his arms around Elliot and said, "Do not worry, he will return to normal when we break the evil dentist's spell, but for now we must leave him behind. Elliot raised a slight smile at the thought of Henry being saved, and he stopped crying, wiping away the last tear from his eye.

"Time to get those sails down", shouted Captain Rosa. She undid the rope at the base of the first mast. The first sail unfolded. "Now tie those two ropes to the side of the ship", said, Captain Rosa. Defender and Patch tied the first sail. Then they moved to the second mast, undid the second sail, and tied it to the side of the ship. The ship started to move, as the wind blew against the sails. Captain Rosa took to the helm of the ship, steering it away from land. "There is a small island a couple of miles away, we can take on provisions there for our journey", said captain Rosa. (Provisions being food and water). Elliot sat at the side of the ship, watching the waves brush along the side of the ship, as it moved through the sea. And every so often, the spray from the waves would land on Elliot's face. And when it did, he licked it up. After half an hour, they were nearing an Island. "Pull up the sails," Shouted Captain Rosa. Defender and Patch undid the ropes and pulled them, the sails rose upwards into bundles. Defender and Patch then tied the ropes to the base of the mast. The ship drifted slowly towards the Shaw. Captain Rosa dropped the anchor into the sea. The ship stopped a couple of meters from land. Captain Rosa then dropped a plank down, creating a bridge from the ship to the island. "Right, everyone. Grab a barrel each and follow me," said Captain Rosa. She walked along the plank, and followed a small stream, up into the hills. The walk did not last long, about ten minutes when Captain Rosa spoke, "Here will do". they had stopped at the bottom of a small waterfall. Captain Rosa filled up two barrels up from the waterfall. But this was no ordinary waterfall, it was cola. She sealed the two barrels and told the others to fill the remaining barrels with fruit from the nearby trees. Elliot and his Friends filled the barrels with fruit. "What do these taste of?", asked Elliot. Captain Rosa replied, "An apple tastes like a pear, a pear tastes like an orange, an orange tastes like a banana, a banana tastes like a peach, and a peach tastes like an apple". "Cool," said Elliot. As soon as the barrels were full, they were heading back to the ship. The journey back was slow with the barrels being very heavy, they carried them with their hands except for Cuddles who carried it on his back. Once back at the ship, they loaded the barrels into the hold, and set sail again, this time towards jelly bear lands. "The journey will take almost a day to reach our destination", said Captain Rosa. After about two hours the wind started to change direction, it was blowing towards them from where they were heading, sending them backwards, the sky was getting very grey, and then out of nowhere was a very dark and nasty cloud, it blew at the ship sending it even further backwards. "Quick, pull up the sails", shouted Captain Rosa. Patch and Defender pulled up the sails as fast as they could. Captain Rosa dropped the anchor so the ship would not go back any further. "that is the evil cloud of the east wind, and with him blowing against us we won't be going anywhere soon", said Captain Rosa. "What do we do now", asked Elliot, with a worried look. "don't worry, I have a plan", said Captain Rosa. The captain headed towards her cabin and returned with a shiny long, purple shell. She placed one end in the sea, and blew into the other. "What is that", asked Elliot. "it's a telephone," replied Captain Rosa. "a telephone, who have you called," asked Elliot. "Just wait and see", said Captain Rosa. Four hours passed and they were still in the same place. "it's time for lunch", said Captain Rosa. They all tucked into the fruit and drank some of the cola from the barrels. All of a sudden there was a tapping from the side of the ship. They all looked all over the side. There was a mermaid. "Hello Rosa," spoke the mermaid. Rosa replied, Hi Princess Lulabel, can you help us, we are trying to reach Jelly Bear lands, and the evil east wind is preventing us from reaching our destination." "I'll get Blue, he will be able to pull you all the way there," said Princess Lulabel the mermaid. And with that she disappeared beneath the sea. "who's Blue," asked Elliot. "he is the biggest mammal of the sea' he is a blue whale, and a giant one", replied Captain Rosa. They waited and waited, and just when it was getting dark, Lulabel the mermaid and Blue turned up. "Hello Rosa," said blue. "Can you help us reach jelly bear lands", asked Rosa. Blue replied, "of course, throw me the end of your rope and ill tow you all the way there. "Thank you ", said Rosa. She then threw down a rope, and Blue took hold of it in his mouth and started to tow the ship towards jelly bear lands. Rosa pulled up the anchor and thanked Lulabel for her help. Seeing the ship being towed, made the east wind angry, and he blew as hard as he could, and no matter how hard he tried he could not stop the ship. "it's time for us all to get some rest, now it's night-time", said Patch. "let's all get bunked up in the cabin," said Captain Rosa. She headed down into the cabin, followed by the others. The cabin had a string of hammocks tied across the ship. They all climb into the hammocks, all except cuddles who choose to sleep on the floor. After about half an hour they were all fast asleep.

The night had passed by, and the sun was shining through the ship window, when all of a sudden there was a large bump, and the ship rocked side to side, swinging the hammocks, and cuddles rolled across the floor. This woke everyone up, and they all ran up the ladder to the top deck. As they looked over the side, they could see land. "you're here, I hope you didn't mind the bump to the side, thought you'd all want to wake. Blue had towed them throughout the night without stopping. "thank you blue", said Captain Rosa. "you're welcome," said Blue. And with that, he disappeared beneath the waves.

"Well, we have reached our destination, and this is where I must leave you, I'll stay here and guard the ship, for your journey home", said Captain Rosa. "Thank you", said Elliot and his friends. Captain Rosa lowered the plank onto the land. Elliot and his friends crossed onto land.

Looking around Elliot thought Jelly Bear Lands looked a lot like the pictures of the holiday destinations, which were in his dad's travel magazines. The beach was pristine white, with bushes, and large trees resembling palm trees, beginning where the beach ends. He remembered wildlife programs in similar places, with lots of noise from parrots, and all other kinds of wild birds. But here, everything was silent, the only thing that could be heard was the sound of Elliot and his friends as they made their way towards the trees.

They approached the trees, and even within the midst of the trees, everything was still silent. "why is this place called, jelly bear lands?", asked Elliot.
Defender replies, "Well it is called it because this is where the giant jelly bears live!".
Jelly Bears might not seem that big, but they are about 6" feet tall. That is about as big as the average dad. But if you were to compare them to the tiny little jelly bears you buy from the sweet shop, then these in the jelly bear lands do look like giants.

As they passed further through the trees, everything was becoming more dense, just like a tropical rainforest. They had been walking for an hour, and still no change.

"Are we going in the right direction?", asked Cuddles. Elliot replies, "Yes, the map shows that we should keep going in the direction of the moon!".

Five minutes later they came across a giant jelly bear. "Oh no," said Patch. They all looked in horror. The bear was no longer 6" feet tall, he was only half the size, of where you would expect his waste to be, anything that was below, had now gone. Melted away. You could see a large sticky puddle around the bear. "don't eat anything, I know what this is, the land is poisoned!," said Patch. And with that, he took a branch from a tree, and snapped it in half. It was rotten inside. "don't eat or drink anything, except for what is in the satchels. We won't find anything living from here onwards!", said Patch. For the group, finding out everything was rotten, was quite fortunate at this time, as they were all starting to get hungry. "Speaking of eating, I'm hungry!" said Elliot. "Me too!" said cuddles. They shared half the food and drink from one of the satchels.

After they had eaten, they continued on their journey. As they walked for the next seven hours, they found countless, lifeless bears on their way. With each sighting, Elliot and his friends were filled with a greater sadness, and a more determined purpose to reach and succeed in their goal of defeating the evil dentist.

After walking for several hours, they were all very tired. "we must stop and rest", said Patch. They all lay in a circle, and one by one, they all fell asleep.

After a very long sleep, Elliot woke and began to wake the others. Once they were all awake, they had breakfast, finishing off what was left in the first satchel. "come on, let's get walking", said Patch.

As they walked, there was more of the same, complete silence, and bear after bear lay lifeless. After about an hour, they were at the end of Jelly Bear Lands. No more trees. In front of them lay miles of swamplands.

If they thought jelly bear lands had been long and strenuous to walk, they had not seen anything yet for the swamplands where unforgiving, pathways twisting and turning as they passed in and out of the swamps. The swamps were toxic. Just a sip would send you to sleep.

"We need to be careful now, one false step, and you will be in the swamp, and if that happens, there won't be anything we can do," said patch. This made Elliot and the others very scared. A good thing that it did. As it encouraged them to be respectful of what was before them and to encourage them to be more careful, so as not to end their lives in such a horrible way, should they slip into the swamps.

Elliot stood and looked before him, took out his map and said, "We need to find the right path through the swamps. The map says there should be a stone marker at the beginning of the path that we should take, it looks a bit like a bear". "I can't see one from here", said

Cuddles. "Neither can I", said Defender. "we must split up, and search for it", said Patch. "I'll go east with Defender and Patch you go south with Cuddles. If either of us has not found it within an hour, we should meet up back here", said Elliot. "Good idea," replied Patch.

Elliot drew an x on the ground so that they would know where to meet back up. The two groups headed their separate ways. After an hour of searching, Patch and Cuddles stopped. "It must be over an hour by now, maybe the others have found it", said Patch. And with that, they turned around to head back to where they started.

Elliot and Defender were having no luck in finding it either. "it's been over an hour, and we have not found it, maybe the others have", said Defender. "You are probably right, but what if they have not, we should give it another five minutes", said Elliot. And with, that they continued onwards. Five minutes passed, and they had not found it. "Well, that five minutes", said Elliot. "Wait, I see something in the distance, over there", said Defender. "your right, I see something, let's go", said Elliot. They both ran as fast as they could. And as they got closer, the object in the distance grew larger. "it's a stone, it's a stone", shouted Elliot. As they were almost next to it, Elliot looked at it. "well, it is a stone, but it does not look like a bear", said Elliot. They both looked in disbelief. "Wait a minute", said Defender, and he headed to the other side of the stone. "it is, it is a bear", said Defender. Elliot rushed to the other side of the stone. And to his amazement, there it was a great big giant of a bear, carved into the other side of the stone. Next to it was a path that headed off into the distance. "We must hurry back to the others and tell them what we have found", said Elliot. They both ran as fast as they could.

They ran so fast, that they had got back to the x, before Cuddles and Patch. They were both incredibly tired having run for so long. Elliot lay on the floor to catch his breath. Five minutes later, Defender could see Patch and Cuddles in the distance. As Patch and Cuddles got closer, Elliot shouted out, "We found it, we found it". Patch and cuddles jumped up into the air in excitement. Elliot picked himself up off the floor. "let's be on our way," said Elliot. And the four friends headed towards the stone.

Having walked such a long way, they were all feeling a little exhausted, and because of this, getting to the stone carving took a little bit longer. Two whole hours!

"We made it", said Patch. they all sat on the floor for a while to get some rest, and to eat and drink, the last food and water from the first satchel. "I hope it won't take us much further, we don't have much drink and food left now", said Cuddles. "Hopefully not long. Having rested, they all got to their feet and looked at the path ahead. It went straight into the distance as far as you could see, it was no wider than about 4ft, and either side was surrounded by swamp water. And in the distance there appeared to be fog covering the swamp and the path that ran through it.

"Well, let's go", said Elliot. And they all walked on down the path through the swamps. As they left the stone carving behind, they noticed, the smell of the rotting swamp, and the further they went the smell grew stronger. every so often scattered throughout the swamps, they would come across jelly bears rotting in the swamps.

After about an hour, they could hardly see where they were going, the fog that they could see earlier so far away, was now covering the path, and the further they went, the thicker the fog became. As they walked, Elliot, Defender, and Patch were talking about what they would do when they defeat the Evil Dentist. Cuddles however could not think about the future, for he was too sad about what had happened, and walked ahead of the others.

An hour later, Defender, Elliot, and Patch were still talking about what they would do, when they heard a tremendous splash, hearing this they ran in the direction of the noise. As they got close, they could see something bobbing up and down in the swamp. Defender quickly reached out his arms to stop Elliot and Patch, for he just managed in time to notice the path had just changed its route, and was heading to the right. "it's Cuddles," screamed Elliot. tears streamed down his face. It was, it was indeed Cuddles, he was upside down with his feet in the air.

Patch dropped to his knees. He was heartbroken. The swamp had taken Cuddles away. Defender hugged Elliot and said, "We must go on, we can't stop now." Patch stood up and said, "your right, we must keep moving". "he must have just walked off the edge, thinking that the path goes straight", said Defender.

The three remaining friends continued, but this time walking slower, so as not to end with the same fate as cuddles, and the many others that the swamp has claimed. They continued further down the path for two more hours, and then the path changed direction again, and then after another two hours, the three of them stopped. "it must be about night-time right now, we should get some sleep before we go any further", said Patch.

They lay sideways on the path with Patch on one side, Defender on the other side, and Elliot in the middle.

The journey was taking its toll on the three of them, this was shown by how fast they all fell asleep, almost immediately.

Several hours later, the three of them began to wake, one after the other, until eventually, they were all wide awake. Patch and Defender sat up, whilst Elliot stood up and outstretched his arms, and yawned. "I needed that sleep", Elliot said. "Me too," said Defender. "So did I", said patch.

As they all looked around, they noticed that the fog had gone completely. And that they were only about ten meters from the end of the path. Which at the end was the beginning of honeycomb mountains. The mountains were incredibly high. Made from layers of milk chocolate, and honeycomb. With the sides spread with chocolate covered with nuggets, and boulders made of gold honeycomb of all sizes. And every so often, honeycomb boulders of various sizes would come crashing down the sides of the mountains.

Defender looked on in disbelief, thinking of the fact that the three of them had to climb this mountain. "is there not an easier way than this", said Defender. Elliot replies, "I'll look at my map." He takes out his map and looks at it long and hard. Elliot says, "The only way is to climb up and go across the tops of the mountains, as the mountains go either way for miles".

"if we must, we must", said Patch. And with that, he starts to climb the side of the mountain. Shortly followed by Defender and Elliot. "Well at least it's not as slippery as ice cream mountains", said Elliot.

After about ten minutes of climbing the mountain, there was a huge rumble under their feet, shortly followed by boulders crashing down the mountain. One of which was heading straight towards the three of them. "quick, get behind the large rock", shouted patch to Elliot and Defender. And they only just managed to get behind it in time. The large boulder that was coming towards them had just crashed into the rock they were standing behind. It shattered into pieces, sending debris down the mountain either on side of the rock. "That was lucky," said Defender. As they climbed further, Patch showed signs of tiring, he was becoming incredibly weak due to a lack of food, and he was starving from not having eaten for some time. The journey up the mountain took a lot longer than it took them to climb ice cream mountains. Every so often throughout their climb they had to stop and wait behind giant boulders, and underneath ridges, due to the repeated landslides of honeycomb pieces falling down the mountainside.

Eventually, the three of them reached the top, and just as they had patch dropped to his knees, before collapsing to the floor. Defender and Elliot rushed to his side. Elliot was screaming out, "Patch, don't give up, please, please Patch". tears run down Elliot's face. Patch spoke quietly, "I can't go on I'm too weak, Defender make sure you get Elliot to the dentist. And Elliot, the only way to beat him is to imagine". and with that Patch fell into a deep sleep. Elliot dropped to his knees, crying uncontrollably. Defender stood alongside Elliot and placed Elliot's head against himself to comfort Elliot.

After about fifteen minutes Elliot stopped crying. Defender speaks quietly, "We must go on, where not far from the evil dentist, look." Elliot turned and looked beyond. There it was the evil dentist's castle in the distance. And between Elliot, Defender and the evil dentist's castle was a series of miniature canyons strewn with many twists and turns, and lots of caves of various sizes. The canyon was a mixture of browns in color, and crumbly in texture. "Were almost there," said Elliot. "Yes, yes we are," said Defender. The two of them climbed down into one of the canyons and made their way towards the castle. Everything was eerie, completely silent, as if everything was dead. The two of them made their way steadily. After about an hour they had reached the end of the canyons. They were within touching distance of the castle. Between them and the castle is a small stretch of flat dusty brown land, and a moat of some kind of toxic substance. The castle is immense, bigger than they had ever imagined. The castle is ten stories high. Built on a base seven floors high. The base and castle are made from the strongest chocolate concrete. The castle reflected that of a French chateaux with towers, windows, and balconies. And there was a sugar dragon, wrapped around one of the castles towers. A sugar dragon breathes out pure icing sugar. If you were to be hit by it, you would start to rot from the sugar, in the same way your teeth rot from eating too many sweets, only one thousand times faster. Not the kind of dragon you would want to mess with.

"That dragon looks scary", said Elliot. "It is," replied Defender. "well, it's a good job that it is sleeping, let's go before he wakes", said Elliot. They both ran towards the castle and stopped at the edge of the toxic moat. "how do we get across" asked Elliot. "I have an idea", replied Defender. He tied the remaining piece of licorice rope to his sword, and the other end to a large licorice root sticking out of the ground. He threw his sword as fast and hard as he could to the other side of the moat. The sword hit a small piece of land at the base of the castle. Defender threw it so hard; it drove straight into the ground. "Wait here Elliot, whilst I check to see if the rope and sword will hold our weight", said Defender. Defender then wrapped his legs around the rope, and pulled himself along it with his hands, until he reached the other side. Once at the other side, he waved Elliot on to cross the rope. Elliot crossed over in the same way that Defender had. Once Elliot was across the rope, Defender pulled out his sword and cut off as much rope as he could. Defender looked up at the castle, and said "What do we do now". "I have an idea", replied Elliot. Having just seen Defender drive his sword into the ground, reminded him of when he was at school, eating his school pudding. Which was chocolate concrete and pink custard. He used to stick his fork into it so he could break it. "We could use your sword and shield to climb up the side of the castle, by sticking them into the side of it, one after the other like rock climbing", said Elliot. "good idea" there are little ledges every so often up the side of the castle, ill climb up to each ledge, then ill pull you up until we get to the top", said Defender. Defender then tied one end of the rope to himself, and the other end to Elliot, and began to climb up the side of the castle. It was slow climbing, but at least Elliot's idea of sticking the shield and sword into the castle worked. It took Defender five minutes to get to the first ledge, which was about twenty feet from the ground, and once he was there, he pulled Elliot up to the ledge. They both continued to climb like that for about two hours until eventually, they were on the last ledge, which was about five feet below the first balcony of the castle. Once there they both rested for a moment, after all climbing up the side of the castle was hard work. "we need to continue, climb onto my shoulders and climb up the balcony", said Defender. Elliot climbed up onto Defender's back and was just reaching over the ledge when he knocked a glass globe from the balcony onto the floor, and it smashed into pieces, making a loud noise. The noise woke the sugar dragon, who immediately flew down, around the base of the castle, and started to circle back up. Defender and Elliot heard the roar of the dragon and looked down in the direction of the dragon. And as they did the dragon looked up in their direction, and as soon he did, he could see Elliot and Defender, and flew upwards towards them as fast as he could. Seeing the dragon move towards them, Elliot said, "Oh no, what do we do?". "leave it to me", replied Defender. He jumped off the ledge with his sword in his hands. Only seconds went by, and he was in touching distance of the dragon. he thrust his sword forward and pierced the dragon's ice-white scales and through the dragon's heart. The dragon screamed. His wings went stiff, and he fell backwards towards the ground. Defender having just killed the dragon was also falling to the ground. Defender turned around as he fell to face Elliot. "YOU MUST GO ON!", shouted Defender to Elliot. The dragon landed in the mote, making a giant splash, followed by Defender shortly afterwards. They both disappeared below the surface. Elliot having just seen his friend fall, pulled himself up from the ledge and over the top into the castle and fell onto the floor. He did not fall far the floor was six feet below the ledge. Even though he saw his friend fall, Elliot did not show any signs of being upset, it's probably because, over the past few days, he has lost many friends. And all that he is thinking about is defeating the dentist.

Elliot looked around, he was in a small room with chocolate concrete walls, and an arched door made out of chocolate fingers. But what he did not expect to see, was crows, lots of crows. But don't worry, Elliot is not in danger for they had all come to the same fate as many of the others of the land, they were all in a deep sleep, having eaten the rotten food around the castle, for having no other food to eat.

Elliot walked slowly towards the door, silently so as not to make any noise in letting the Evil Dentist know that he was there. Elliot made his way up to the great hall, through narrow corridors and spiral staircases.

Elliot was nearing the great hall when he heard a voice, it was the Evil Dentist. Elliot peeped out from behind the door. The great hall is vast, with vertical columns surrounding the hall, supporting the ceiling above. The spell castor was walking in circles talking to himself, "Where is he, where is he." The Evil Dentist sounded frustrated. Looking up at the ceiling, Elliot noticed that there was a cage tied to the ceiling, and inside were his friends Ginger and Rolie, who were captured earlier. They were fast asleep, under the spell of the Evil Dentist. And even though his friends could not help, and that he was all alone, Elliot had somehow found the courage to face the Evil Dentist on his own. He was no longer afraid.

Elliot stepped out from behind the doorway and walked towards the Evil Dentist. "Looking for me", said Elliot. The Evil Dentist turned around, surprised by hearing Elliot's Voice. "so you have come to face me at last", said the Evil Dentist. In an instant, the Evil Dentist clapped his hands, and out of nowhere the room started to fill with Grongels, they were pouring through the windows, and the doors, there were hundreds of them, and they filled the great hall. Everywhere Elliot looked, there were Grongels. The evil dentist spoke, "You see, you cannot defeat me." "I am not afraid", said Elliot. "we will see", replied the Evil Dentist. And with that, he clapped his hands again, and the Grongels marched towards Elliot.

Elliot fought bravely, but there were to many. He pulled many Grongels apart, but eventually, Elliot was being held down by them. The Evil Dentist lowered the cage to the floor by undoing the rope that was holding it up at the top of the ceiling. Once the cage was on the floor, the Grongels carried Elliot and placed him inside the cage. The Evil Dentist pulled the rope, and the was again at the top of the ceiling. The evil dentist laughed and said, "You have lost, you could never have beaten me". Elliot sat there in the cage thinking about what he could do, then he remembered what Patch said to him, "Use your imagination, which is the only way you will defeat the dentist". Elliot thought to himself, "Imagine, imagine, imagine what". Elliot then remembered the time that he was having a snowball fight with his sisters, and at the time he imagined that the snowballs were sticky bombs and that when they hit someone they were stuck still, not being able to move. He used his imagination, and right then in both his hands were two sticky snow balls, and the more he imagined the more he had. There was now a pile of sticky snowballs on the floor of his cage. Elliot looked around at all the Grongels who were all around the great hall. Elliot started to throw sticky snowballs at the Grongels, Splat, Splat, they hit the Grongels. Elliot kept throwing one after the other. The Grongels could not move, they were stuck still. The Evil Dentist was shocked at what he saw. His Grongels were being defeated. This made the Evil Dentist Angry. The Evil Dentist shouted at his Grongels, "Get him." but it was too late. All the Grongels were now stuck and could not move. "the Evil Dentist shouted, "It does not matter, you are my prisoner, I have still won". hearing this made Elliot more determined than ever. Elliot looked at the cage. The cage was made from chocolate. Elliot remembered at that moment that chocolate does melt. Elliot rubbed the chocolate bars with his hands. The chocolate warmed up and started to melt. First one bar, then two, then three. The Evil dentist could do nothing but look on in disbelief. Once five bars were melted away, Elliot imagined a rope, and it appeared in front of him. Elliot tied one end of the rope to the cage and lowered the other to the floor. Elliot then climbed down the rope, and within an instant he was standing on the floor of the great hall, facing the Evil Dentist. The evil dentist had a magic staff in his hand, and thrust it forward repeatedly. And every time he did magic balls flew towards Elliot. Elliot jumped from one side to the other, and then back again, avoiding the magic balls. The Evil Dentist stopped. Elliot thought to himself, "If I had that magic staff, I could use it on the evil dentist. Elliot reached out his arm. And in an instant, the magic staff was now in Elliot's hand. The Evil Dentist was shocked and now afraid. Elliot thrust the magic staff forward, and a magic ball flew out of the staff and hit the Evil Dentist in the chest. There was a sudden purple flash when it hit the Evil Dentist. The was a magical glow spreading outwards all over the Evil Dentist's body. The magic ball froze the Evil Dentist to the spot like a statue. Elliot slammed the staff down on the floor. When it hit the floor, the was a tremendous sound like thunder. A magic glow spread outwards from the staff in all directions. It moved incredibly fast. The world began to glow. The Evil Dentist's spell was broken. Elliot looked up at the cage. Rolie and Ginger were waking from the spell. Everywhere began to smell sweet. All that was rotten inside was now back to normal. Elliot walked across to the wall, untied the rope from the wall that was holding the cage up to the ceiling, and lowered the cage down to the floor. Rolie and Ginger stepped out from the cage through the hole that Elliot made in the cage moments earlier. Harper and Rolie hugged Elliot and Rolie said, "You did it, you did it, I knew you would". all three of them paused for a moment to look at the Evil Dentist who was frozen still. "will he stay like that?", asked Rolie. Elliot replied, "No, eventually he will defrost, but there is no need to worry, he has no more magic, I have his magic staff". "let's go home," said Ginger.

Elliot and his friends made their way back home, meeting up with their other friends on the way. First to be reunited was Defender, second was Patch, third was Cuddles, and last was Henry. Before Elliot went back to his world he stopped by the home of Pipin the Magical. Waiting for him was a surprise celebration, almost all the toys of the land were there. There were banners and balloons. The toys threw a party in celebration of Elliot and his friends and what they had achieved. During the celebrations, Pipin the Magical thanked Elliot for all he had done and said to him, "You can achieve anything in life, all you have to do is believe." Elliot gave Pipin the Magical, the magic staff that used to belong to the Evil Dentist. Pipin the magical thanked Elliot again. And Elliot said, "I must go now, my family will be waiting for me." Elliot and his friends made their way back to the chocolate lagoon, where the magic tunnel led back to Elliot's world. Before climbing back up the wall of the waterfall, Elliot thanked his friends, both new and old, those who were his toys, and his new friends that he met in the world of toys. The toys all took turns to thank Elliot in return. Elliot asked his friends, "Will I see you all again". Patch replied, "When you wake every day we will be in your bedroom waiting for you. There were tears in the eyes of Elliot and his friends when they parted. Elliot climbed the wall of the waterfall and made his way back up the tunnel. Elliot was then magically transported back to his world.

Having just been magically transported back to his world, Elliot found himself waking up in his bed. The sun's rays were just making their way through the gap in the curtain. The sun was just rising in the morning. Elliot looked around his room, nothing was black and white anymore, and everything seemed normal. He jumped off his bed and ran into his sister's room. "Wake up, wake up," shouted Elliot to his sisters. Abigail and Scarlet woke up. "You are awake, you are awake, I can't believe it, you are awake", said Elliot. "of course we are awake, you just woke us up, what is wrong with you", said Scarlet. "I love you both very much, I have missed you", said Elliot. Scarlet and Abigail thought their brother was being weird. Elliot ran downstairs to the kitchen, where his dad was. His father had just cooked a fried breakfast for everyone. Upon seeing his father, Elliot ran to his dad and wrapped his arms around his dad, saying "I love you, Dad". his father wrapped his arms around Elliot, and replied "I love you too, now go get your breakfast". Elliot sat down to eat his breakfast. His two sisters came downstairs shortly afterwards and sat down to eat their breakfast. Elliot was halfway through eating his breakfast when his father said, "Do not forget, you are at the dentist today. Hearing this Elliot remembered the evil dentist. Elliot paused for a moment. He looked around the room at everything. And then he thought to himself, "was it just a dream, my toys, Pipin the magical, the evil dentist.

Elliot's father spoke, "When you three have finished your breakfast, go get ready for school, your school clothes have been ironed, and they are on my bed ready for you". Elliot and his two sisters finished their breakfast and went upstairs to get ready for school. Shortly after the three of them returned downstairs to their father. Elliot's father picked up the car keys, and said, "let's go, Ill drop you two girls off at school, and then I'll take you to the dentist Elliot. Elliot felt nervous, he had never been to a dentist before, and he was scared of them.

They all got in the car and drove off. After about fifteen minutes they were at the school. Their father got out of the car walked around the other side, and opened the door to let Abigail and Scarlet out. Their father gave them both a kiss, and said, "You too have a nice day, and I'll pick you both up from school, love you both". they both ran off and into their school.

Elliot's father got back into the car. "Right let's go get to the dentist", said Elliot's father, and he then drove Elliot to the dentist. They pulled up outside the dentist's surgery. Elliot's father got out of the car first, followed by Elliot. They both walked down the path to the surgery. Elliot's father opened the door for Elliot. Elliot walked inside to the waiting room. Elliot's father walked to the desk and spoke to the receptionist, "Hi, I am George Summer, I have brought my son, Elliot Summer to see the dentist". the receptionist replied, "We have been expecting you, take a seat and we will call you through to see the dentist soon". George Summer and Elliot sat down in the waiting area. While they waited Elliot was looking around the room, and he noticed a box of toys in the corner of the room. To his astonishment there in the box were toys that looked exactly like Defender and Cuddles. At that moment the receptionist called out, "The Dentist will see you now Elliot, it is the first door on the right down the corridor, walk straight in. Elliot and his dad walked into the room where the dentist was. Elliot had to look twice, the dentist looked just like the dentist in his dream. "come sit down", said the dentist to Elliot. Elliot sat back in the dentist's chair. "Right, lay back, and open your mouth wide so we can take a look", said the Dentist to Elliot. Elliot laid back and opened his mouth. The dentist took out a small mirror and placed it into Elliot's mouth. The Dentist examined Elliot's teeth. "I see, I see, we have a rotten tooth at the back, not to worry, it is only a baby tooth, we will have it out in no time, we will give you a small injection to numb the pain, and then we will take it out", said the Dentist. The Dentist took a needle from a small metal tray on the side. "You will feel a small prick, it will a hurt a little, and then your mouth will go numb, and then we will be able to remove your tooth", said the dentist. The dentist placed the needle into Elliot's mouth, and injected a small amount into Elliot's gum, just below the rotten tooth. It did indeed hurt a little. "We will wait five minutes for your gum to go numb, and then we will remove it", said the dentist. Elliot laid waiting in the chair for five minutes. And after the five minutes, his gum was indeed numb. "Is your mouth numb yet?", asked the Dentist. "Elliot replied as best he could, for he could hardly speak properly with a numb mouth, "yes". The Dentist picked up his tool. It looked like small pliers. He placed it into Elliot's mouth and took hold of Elliot's rotten tooth. And in an instant, he pulled the tooth right out of Elliot's mouth. "there you go, all done, you can rinse your mouth out with that cup of water there", said the dentist. Elliot rinsed out his mouth, and got down out of the chair. "we will see you in six months for a check, it was nice to see you again", said the dentist, and smiled.

Elliot and his father left the dentist and walked to the car. Elliot thought to himself, "Again?, I haven't been to the dentist before!".

Was it just a dream, or did it happen after all?